Project Nemesis

Project Nemesis

Chad Gunter

Acrasia Media

CONTENTS

PROJECT NEMESIS

Published by Acrasia Media
Charlotte, North Carolina

This book is a work of fiction. Some of the characters, events, and places portrayed in this book are fictitious. Some of the characters, however, are based upon real people and their similarities and characteristics are used with their permissions. Any other similarities to real persons, living or dead, is coincidental, and not intended by the author.

Cover graphic design copyright a-papatoniou

Publisher's Cataloging-in-Publication data

Names: Gunter, Chad Eric, author.
Title: Project Nemesis / Chad Eric Gunter.
Description: Charlotte, NC: Acrasia Media, 2022.
Identifiers: ISBN: 978-1-958202-04-3 (hardcover) | 978-1-958202-10-4 (paperback) | 978-1-958202-07-4 (ePub)
Subjects: LCSH Nanotechnology--Fiction. | Science--Experiments--Fiction. | Human experimentation in medicine--Fiction. | Genetic engineering--Fiction. | Science fiction. | BISAC FICTION / Science Fiction / General | FICTION / Science Fiction / Action & Adventure | FICTION / Science Fiction / Genetic Engineering
Classification: LCC PS3607 .U4815 P76 2022 | DDC 813.6--dc23

Second Printing, 2022

Wednesday, August 12th

A tall, slender man, with brown hair, wearing jogging shorts and a black hard rock t-shirt walked through the front glass doors of the fitness center. He beeped in with his membership card that was attached to his keychain, and then hung his keys up on the pegboard next to the door. "Hi, Alan." said one of the employees at the front desk. He waved and proceeded forward into the gym. As he walked by the lounge area, he made eye contact with someone seated at one of the tables. He was shorter than Alan, but was also slender. Unlike Alan, who was sporting a full beard – which was a rarity for him - he had a full goatee, which currently needed grooming. He was holding his hat in his hand, revealing a bald head, except for fuzz on the sides, which was as far as the trimmer would cut. He was also wearing a t-shirt with an old-school rock band logo on it. They immediately exchanged disgusted looks for a few seconds, and then both cracked smiles. Alan said "Alright loser, let's do this." Cord just shook his head.They had been working out together for eight months. Alan had been working out regularly for nearly twenty years. It was Cord's first time, ever. Both men were in their late thirties, and had worked together for fifteen years. One day, at work, Cord had again complained of his weight and feeling tired most of the time. After calling him a big cry baby and asking him to please stop whining, Alan invited him to come with him to the gym and give it a try. In just a few short months of working out, and proper diet, he had lost nearly 45 pounds, and had never felt better in his life. With this newfound confidence, Cord placed health and fitness as one of the top priorities in his life, moving it from somewhere near the bottom of his list.

Although both men were in relatively good health, Alan had been taking care of himself for much longer than Cord, and was much leaner. Neither one, however, had the kind of muscle that you usually would only see in magazines. Both men wanted to increase their size somewhat, and not be as thin. Alan made it no secret that he wanted to get big. Although Cord was happy actually being skinny for the first time in his life, he also liked the idea of gaining some muscle mass. That is why it was day number one of Alan's new workout routine. They had been using a workout routine Alan had created which gave really good results for health and definition. The new routine, coupled with some dietary changes, however, would hopefully allow them to see an increase in muscle mass.

Cord pushed the barbell up one last time for the last rep of the set on the Smith machine. He had never performed a decline bench press before, and his muscles were exhausted.

Alan, who was spotting for him, had to assist the last few inches to place the barbell on the notch. "I think I'll call your new workout routine the *Alan's Pump Up or Die Trying*, also known as the *You'll Sleep Good Tonight Routine.*" They laughed at this and then continued on to their next machine. After completing their last set for the afternoon, the two headed for the fitness center door. Cord noticed a stack of flyers on the counter at the front desk that he had never seen before. He stopped and read the one on top:

Looking for some extra $$$ for doing something you love to do anyway? We need participants for a clinical trial using a radically different muscle-building supplement and some outstanding training techniques. Only serious individuals who are willing to work hard to see major improvements in themselves need apply. No illegal drug users of any kind will be accepted, and we will be testing. If you feel you already have significant muscle mass from previous weight training, please do not apply at this time. This is a study for the effectiveness of our program on average individuals who have an interest in weight training. Please call 704-555-0101 to schedule an appointment.

Cord picked up two copies of the flyers and handed one to Alan. Alan crumpled it into a ball and launched it into Cord's forehead. "Wait, clown –" Cord said, retrieving the crumpled paper back up off of the floor and handing it back to him. "I'm just kidding." Alan said, straightening out the paper. "What's this boolcrap all about?" he added. "This sounds perfect! Just what we've been looking for!" Cord said, excitedly. Alan read the paper and simply frowned. "Ehhhhh. . ." he finally said. "Well, I know I'm usually skeptical about stuff like this, too.

But, for one – there's money involved, and I sure could use some extra. Two, from the way I take it, we'd still be working out. And three, it mentioned *products*, which is most likely some new brand of protein shake, creatine or something – which of course, we'd be getting for free. I think you know how I feel about free stuff by now, right?" said Cord, grinning. They had already walked out into the parking lot of the fitness center, and were standing by their cars. "I don't guess it'd hurt to give it a try. If it turns out to be a bunch of garbage, we'll just give 'em the ole California howdy." Alan said. "That's how we roll, right?" said Cord. Alan smiled at Cord's attempt at sounding cool. Alan thought his buddy was 'cool,' but in much different ways.

2 |

Friday, August 14th

A couple of days later, on Friday, the two friends met for lunch at a restaurant local to their work area in Charlotte, North Carolina. "I called that place." Cord said. Alan finished a bite of his sandwich. "What place?" he asked. "You remember those flyers I picked up at the gym." He responded. "Oh, crap, you're not really going to fool with that bogus mess, are you?" Alan said, rhetorically, as he rolled his eyes. "Well . . . yeah . . . and I thought you were interested in giving it a try, too." he said. "Nahh, I don't need whatever they got." Alan said. "Man, the place is just right down the road, off of South Boulevard, here in Charlotte. I also told the lady I talked to about you and I . . ." Cord began. "And now, she thinks we're *both* a couple of weirdos." Alan interrupted. "No, listen," Cord said frustrated. "I told her about how you and I have been working out together for eight months, and you've been the one who has really helped me get into shape . . . you've been working out for nearly twenty years, and I have for only eight months. Although we're both in pretty good shape, neither one of us really has gained the kind of muscle mass that we would like and we want to do something about it." Cord finished. Alan kept looking at Cord, waiting. "She said that it sounded as if we would both be perfect candidates for their clinical study. One of us who has only been working out for a short while, and the other for several years, and neither with any substantial muscle mass. She really sounded like she would accept both of us for the study, but we have to go down there and speak with her in person and fill out an application or something." He waited for Alan to say something. When Alan did not volunteer any further comment, Cord said "Come on, it'll just take a few minutes and it's close by." Alan shook his head, smiling, and said "You're always working some kind of angle on something."

The address led them to a building that looked more like an industrial warehouse than the small office that both men had been expecting. There was a guard house at the gate. There was a tall chain link fence with barbed wire on top of it – not uncommon for industrial warehouses in the area. The building was plain except for a six-bay loading dock, several parking areas, and a couple of standard sized doors at the end of each parking area. Alan shot Cord a quick text "Are we here to fill out an application, or visit an inmate?" Cord responded "No joke, they must serve one heck of a protein shake." Cord was the first one to the gate. The guard was very polite. "Can I help you?" he asked. "Yes, I'm here to see Doctor Lawson about the clinical study." He answered. "Name please?" the guard asked. "Cord Grayson." He replied. The guard looked over his clipboard and then said "Go to parking area D. The entrance will be labeled corresponding to the parking area." The powered chain link gate began to roll back. Alan stopped and gave his name and then followed Cord to the parking area.

Parking area D was the only parking area that had cars in it. If not for that fact, the warehouse would have looked otherwise abandoned. They approached the door labeled *"D"* and Cord reached out and turned the knob. It would not open. A man's voice boomed out of a talk box next to the door. "Yes?" Cord identified himself and Alan. The door buzzed and he pulled it open. As they came into the gloomy hallway and rounded the corner, there was a security checkpoint with a guard behind a glass window. They were asked to leave their phones with the guard. They reluctantly did so. The guard waved and another door was buzzed open for them. "Are you sure we're supposed to be here?" Alan asked.

They were in another drab hallway that had a single office on the left. On the door was a sign labeled "Receptionist." There was another door at the end of the hallway labeled "Authorized Personnel Only" with a data card reader next to it. They walked toward the receptionist's office. She was on the phone, but saw them through the window on the door and used her hand to motion to them to come in. "Okay, we'll expect those by Thursday, then. Thank you." she said to someone on the phone and then hung up. "Hi, gentlemen. My name is Beverly Withers and I am the receptionist for this facility. I know you two, but I don't know which is which." Cord offered his hand to her and they shook. he said "I'm

Cord, the good one." She smiled. "Yeah, good for nothing. I'm Alan." said Alan as he shook her hand, the three of them laughing. "Let me call Doctor Lawson and let her know you guys are here." Beverly picked up the phone. "Doctor Lawson, the two men are here about the clinical study." She hung up the phone and said "She'll be right in."

Doctor Andrea Lawson was beautiful. She had long, curly, sandy blonde hair. You could still make out her perfect figure under her white lab coat. After introductions were made all around, Alan said "Okay, now where do we sign up?" Cord rolled his eyes and shook his head. "Let me go over our program and then you can make up your mind. Basically, you'll keep on doing what you've been doing already. You'll be working out at your convenience, but you'll no longer be taking any of your dietary or fitness supplements, such as creatine, protein, et cetera. In fact, I'd like for your diet to be as average as possible. I'm not saying to eat greasy cheeseburgers all of the time, but don't worry so much if you don't have the grilled chicken every day." She began. "But if that's what we like, it's okay, right?" Cord asked. "Yes. I'm just saying don't go out of your way or actively pursue extreme healthy eating. The purpose of our clinical study is to see what our performance enhancers will do for the fairly average individuals who are eating fairly typical - which oftentimes means somewhat unhealthy - meals." She replied. "So, what are the secret ingredients to these enhancers?" Alan asked. "Sorry, you actually said it - it's a trade *secret*. Let's just say that they are much more potent and can do more for you than your standard amino acids, creatine, or even anabolic steroids." Alan's eyes widened. "Yes, I thought that would grab your attention." she said. "Are their risks or side effects?" Cord asked. Doctor Lawson sighed, and hopped up onto the corner of Beverly's desk, her legs swinging. "Well, as with any medications, there are risks and possible side effects. We've been working on this program for several years, now. There, of course, have been side effects. But, over the years, we have refined the formula, and the risks and the possibility of side effects have been dramatically reduced. Most of the possible side effects are not much different than the ones you could have with a cocktail of some of your standard meds you'd receive from antibiotics and so forth, such as headache, diarrhea, and nausea. Only a few of our participants had these side effects, and they subsided after a few weeks." she said. The two men nodded their heads in understanding. "So, you would consider us as average, huh?" Cord asked. "You two . . ." she began. "Clowns?" Alan interjected. She smiled. "You two *guys*" she said, enunciating the word guys from Alan's word play "are above average, when it comes to health and fitness. We have a variety of individuals in the study. These people range from the obese, who are in poor health, all the way up to body-builders who always eat right and exercise frequently, but indeed have been using steroids, amongst other illegal body building products. We are studying the effectiveness of our performance enhancers on a variety of people who live a variety of lifestyles. You two *guys*" she said, enunciating the word guys again "are definitely an interest to me. You seem to be in many ways, a couple of average Joes, who have been pushing your bodies to performance, with only your hard work, determination and possibly some publicly available dietary aids – thus, the *above* average label. That's exactly what we're currently looking for, here. There are a lot of candidates who fit your profiles closely and are available for this program. After getting a good look at you guys, meeting you, and talking to you face-to-face, I'm satisfied that you'd be perfect for the program. So, if you're interested, the spots are yours. Keep in mind, however . . . if you turn it down now, you won't get another opportunity." She finished. The two men exchanged glances, as if asking each other what they thought. After a short pause, Cord asked "I hate to ask, because this sounds pretty good, but exactly how much would we be getting paid to participate in the study?" Andrea turned to him and said "Twenty-five dollars an hour, with a minimum of two hours a day of participation." They exchanged glances again, both of them doing the math in their heads, this time smiling. "What about days that we may have to stay longer at work?" Alan asked. "I'll take care of that." she said. Sensing the doubt and hesitation in the men, she added "You will have a very flexible schedule. There are people working in this facility 24 hours a day who will be able to do the testing. Of course, there will be some days that we will need you all day long. This project is funded by the federal government. If we need you during your regular working hours, we'll take care of it – and you'll still be compensated your regular pay." The two men looked at each other once again. It seemed as though they couldn't lose with this deal. "Okay, I'll ask it again: Where do we sign up?" said Alan.

Dr. Lawson hopped down off of the desk as Beverly Withers pulled out two stacks of papers from one of the file cabinet drawers behind her desk and handed one stack to each of the two men. "I guess I'll see you two *guys* Monday afternoon" Dr. Lawson said, extending her hand. "It was a pleasure meeting you and I look forward to working with you." She added as they all shook hands. She headed to the door and opened it. "Beverly will go over these forms with you" She threw up one hand as a last wave and then stepped out and closed the door. "These are pretty much standard forms. One is for liability, which pretty much goes over the risks and possible side effects in detail and holds us free from any and all liability should anything happen to you. One is for non- disclosure of trade secret information, which is basically an agreement saying that you will not disclose any information about anything you see, hear, feel, smell, or experience in this study – and if you do, you're subject to fine and / or imprisonment. One is a general application where you fill out your name, address, social security number, telephone number, you know, the whole nine yards about yourself. One is for release of your medical records to us. One is a standard contract about what is expected of you in this study, and what payment you have agreed to receive. One is giving us ownership of any biological samples we take from you so that we can use them in the study in any way we see fit. One is to perform additions to your biology as needed, when needed. One is a direct deposit form for your bank." She finished. "Which one gives you ownership of our souls?" Cord asked, jokingly, as they were both overwhelmed with the bombardment of information. "That's the blue contract that I've already mentioned." she said, slyly, with a smile. Alan stood up and Cord followed his lead. "Do we bring these back here, when we're finished with them?" Alan asked. "Oh, you need to go ahead and fill those out before you leave." said Beverly. "It looks like it would take us the rest of the day to read and fill these out." Cord said, automatically reaching for his phone to check the time, before he remembered leaving it with the guards. "Yeah, we have to get back to our jobs. We just swung by here on our way back from lunch." Alan said. "If you'll go ahead and sign the blue contract, you won't have to worry about it. Then you can fill the rest of these out later. I'll take care of your employer." she said.

That afternoon, during their workout at the local fitness center, both men were quiet, except for the brief discussions of their current workout. There were no remarks about the couple of pumped-up guys who walked by and were obviously on steroids. There was not any trash-talking about the atrocious music the fitness center played over and over. There weren't even any comments about attractive women as they would walk by. It was not uncommon for Cord to be moody, sometimes. But it was unlike Alan to ever seem distant. Both men had a feeling of foreboding. After their workout, the men muttered their goodbyes to each other. Cord pulled out of the fitness center parking lot, and headed home. Alan waited to meet his mother who had his two-year old daughter.

3

Monday, August 17th

Both men worked primarily out in the field, but needed to go to their office this morning for some administrative duties. Both men were visited by their supervisors and each had received a similar talk. Their supervisors had informed them that they were aware that they would have to be off from time to time, sometimes with little or no notice. They had said to just call them and let them know, and they would take care of the rest. They bumped into each other in the elevator, leaving the building. "Hey, dork, did your supervisor talk to you about accommodating our clinical study?" Alan asked Cord. "As a matter of fact, he did, dweeb." Cord replied. "Cool." Alan said. They both got off of the elevator smiling from ear to ear. The ominous feeling that they had shared Friday had already faded away.

Alan identified himself to the guard at the gate, and then drove his car to parking area D. He saw Cord was already there, sitting in his car, waiting for him, he supposed. After he parked and got out of his car, Cord did as well. They went through the same door as before and made their way to the receptionist's office, where Beverly was sitting. She waved and buzzed the door labeled *Authorized Personnel Only*. As they walked through the door, the environment changed dramatically. It seemed as if they were no longer in an old warehouse, but in a hospital. They stepped on to a white tiled hallway with white walls. There was the hustle and bustle of activity down the hall and beyond. People wearing white lab coats, walking along, some individually, some paired up, talking numbers and science, carrying clipboards and file folders. There were several caged animals on wheeled carts along the hallway. There were some mice, some cats, some dogs, and even a few monkeys. There were various office doors scattered down both sides of the hallway, all labeled with its function on the doorway. There was a larger door at the end of the hallway, labeled only with red and white cautionary stripes.

Doctor Lawson approached them as they were looking around in awe. "Hi, guys." she said happily. "Hello, Doctor Lawson." Cord said. "Hey." Alan said. "Please call me Andrea. Follow me so we can get started." she said as she turned and headed down the hallway toward one of the offices. They followed her into an office labeled *Primary Care*. There was a man in a lab coat seated at a table, writing in a tablet. He looked up and finished his writing. "Ahh, Andrea. I see you have some new Guinea Pigs for us." he said, smiling at the men, as he picked up one of his clipboards and glanced over the text. He then extended his hand to each of them. "I'm Doctor Kitridge. Mr. Carson, Mr. Grayson." he said as he shook hands in the correct order. "But, please call me Nathan. I'll be taking some blood and giving you two complete physicals today." Cord asked "Is the blood work to check for drug use?" Nathan said "Well, that, and we'll be looking at a whole bunch of other things, as well." Andrea said "Well, I'll leave you two with Nathan. I promise you'll be in good hands." As she closed the door, Doctor Kitridge said "Okay, I'll try to make this as painless as possible. Each of you pick an examining room and go in and undress." He nodded to the small hallway inside his office, lined with several small rooms. "Turds first." said Alan, motioning for Cord to move forward, as he was closer to the hallway anyway. Cord just shook his head and walked forward, taking it that time. "You two have known each other for a while, haven't you?" Asked Nathan. "I don't know this clown." Cord responded.

The examinations and blood collections for the two men took a little more than an hour to complete. As they walked out into the main hallway, Doctor Lawson met them. "Well, that wasn't so bad, was it?" she asked. "Not at all." Cord said. "Well, at least one member of the staff here knows a lot about Cord . . . or should I say very little." Alan said, smiling, holding his thumb and index finger about an inch apart. "Yeah, that same staff member knows that at least one of us has one." Cord retorted, with a smile of his own. "Good one." Alan said, laughing. Doctor Lawson was half-smiling and half-in-shock. "Sorry, Doc. I guess it's a little early for us to be talking like that around you." Alan said. Her smile broadened. "It's okay. It's funny. Most people around here are so dull. It's kind of refreshing, actually. Completely vulgar, but also refreshing."

she said. She started walking toward the door at the beginning of the hallway, where they came in. They walked with her. "Uhh, where are we going to be working out today?" Cord asked. "Oh, today, you don't need to work out. You know, you've had some blood taken and so forth." Cord looked over at Alan. Alan could tell that Cord did not like that answer. "It was just a small amount, we both feel fine." Cord added. "Just go home and get some rest. We've got some more things to do tomorrow." she said a little too sharply. "Sorry, I asked." Cord said. They were both surprised to see Doctor Lawson with that demeanor. She stopped before they reached the door. "No, I'm sorry I snapped. Sometimes, I'm under a lot of pressure here. This project is much more delicate than you would think, and when I need you to follow my directions as far as the program goes, I need to know that you are going to do so. It's the best for everyone, believe me. I know from talking to you and reading your files that you are dedicated to fitness, each for your own reasons, and don't want to miss any opportunities to further your goals." She started. It was as if she was reading their minds. She seemed to know exactly how the men felt about their desires for fitness. "But, you've got to believe me when I say *there will be dramatic changes in your physiques and physical performance.* Any workouts you may miss during this program will not matter. But, you've got to listen to me, and do what I tell you to do. See you tomorrow." She finished, as she pulled the door open for them. "Fair enough." Alan said as they walked through the door.

The next afternoon at the lab, Doctor Lawson led them to another office and introduced the two men to Doctor Patricia

Fielding. She was a psychiatrist who did mental evaluations of the two men. They spent two hours with her going back and forth between the two, who were in private rooms in her office. She gave them several problem-solving tests. She gave them an IQ test. She did the Mandelbrot inkblot test. She delved into their past and personal history. Once the two men were rejoined in the main area of her office, she had the men sit down and she sat down behind her desk. "I just wanted to let you guys know that you have done very well. There are really no right or wrong answers to anything I have questioned you about today." she said. "Even when Alan thought that #23 of the Mandelbrot series was his reflection?" Cord asked, grinning. Doctor Fielding let out a small, professional laugh. Alan said "Tee, hee." unenthusiastically. "I know you were just joking, but I really can't give any comments on either one of your tests – other than what I've already stated. You're free to go. Doctor Lawson is on her way to meet you at the door." As Doctor Lawson stepped in, Doctor Fielding began writing notes in a composition book. "Ok, guys, ready to go?" Andrea asked. The two men stood and followed her through the door. "Nice meeting you." Alan said. "Uhh, huhh." Doctor Fielding said, looking up briefly from her composition book and smiling. As they closed the door behind them Andrea said "I know – she's not very social to be a shrink, huh?" Alan said "She's definitely all business." She led them to the exit and said "See you tomorrow. No need for a workout today." The two men both said "'Bye."

As the two men pulled out of the facility parking lot, through the gate, onto South Boulevard, Cord called Alan.

"This is ludicrous. I'm going to the gym." he said. "My wife has the baby tonight . . . here we go." Alan responded. They went on to their local fitness center and got in their regular Tuesday workout before they headed home.

4

Wednesday, August 19th

Cord and Alan met one of their coworkers for lunch today, as it was a special occasion. It was Alan's birthday. They ate at a little steakhouse where they had eaten before on other occasions. Jason Kaiser was a little taller than Cord, but much more solid from his years of physical labor and working out. His brown hair was usually a little scattered around with hair gel, that he said the women really loved. He was loud, boisterous and he wasn't joking about the women admirers, and there were quite a few. Cord knew his heart, though, and he knew he was more of a teddy bear than he let on, and, he would, however, literally, do just about anything to help a friend.

That afternoon, Doctor Lawson greeted them and wished Alan a happy birthday. She then led them to yet another office down the hallway. In this office, there were quite a few pieces of office equipment and filing cabinets. There was the steady pace of several members of the administrative staff on telephones, making photo copies, filing, and so on. Doctor Lawson approached the counter with the two men following. "Hi, Stanley." she said. A short and stocky young man with hair so blonde, it was almost white, a bowl haircut and thick glasses came to the counter. "Hi, Andrea." he said. "Stanley, I've got these two gentlemen here to have ID / keycard badges made. Give them section 2 clearance on my authority." she said. "Yes ma'am. Follow me, please." he said to Alan and Cord. The two men were photographed and given photographic keycards, similar to the ones they already used at work. They left the administrative office. As they were walking out the door, Andrea said "Okay, although you won't be working out today, I want to give you a little tour of some of the equipment . . ." She was suddenly interrupted by the loud smack of a mop handle falling flat against the floor at the doorway they were using to come into the hall. Everyone jumped, but Cord was the last one through, and an old black man with white hair and a white mustache, wearing green coveralls, stumbled right into him, sending both of them sprawling to the floor. A wheeled mop bucket with a ringer attachment went rolling by. Cord felt as if the man had tried his best to keep him from falling, because he had grabbed his hand as they went down. Doctor Lawson quickly began assisting the man. Alan went to offer his hand to Cord. "Joe! Are you okay?" she asked the old man with concern. "Just a little clumsy, I guess. I'm alright." He muttered. "That's good." she said. She still had a look of concern about her. "Joe, don't you remember you're not supposed to clean the areas in sections 1 & 2 until after 8 pm, when the guest board has mostly cleared? Roberson will get really mad if he were to see you out here, now." she said. "I know, Miss Lawson, I had some cleaning to do in section 3, and remembered that I had left my mop and bucket here in section 1. I'm sorry Miss Lawson." he said, apologetically. "Joe, you know that it doesn't matter to me. And I don't know what the big deal is, really, but you know how Roberson can be." she said. As an afterthought, she asked "Aren't there like twenty of those mops and buckets in sanitation storage areas in each section, anyway?" Joe looked down at his feet, as though embarrassed. "Why yes, Miss Lawson, but this one is my *favorite*." he said, looking back up and grinning. "Sometimes, you're just too much. Please be more careful with yourself, Joe." she said fondly, putting her hand on his shoulder. Old Joe scooted away as fast as he could. They watched Joe as he disappeared through one of the doorways at the end of the hall. Andrea turned to Cord. "Are you okay?" she asked. "Oh, I'm fine. I hope he is." They continued their walk toward the large double-doors with the reflective striping on them at the end of the hallway. "Wanna try out your keycard?" she asked, looking at the two men. Alan swiped his keycard in front of the keypad. There was a small beep, then the doors opened mechanically, swinging inward. They all stepped through into another hallway which was similar to the one they were leaving in section one. There were several doors to several offices on both sides of the hallway. On the left side, however, there was one door that said *Fitness* with a text-style that varied from the other offices, making it stand out. Doctor Lawson proceeded to the door. There were keypads at most of the doors along the hallway, as there was at the gym, but she simply pushed this door open. As they stepped through, the men's eyes widened in amazement. It was huge. There, of course, were many pieces of equipment both men were familiar with, but some, even Alan had never seen before. The pieces were in groups of four. There were several people buddied-up, using machines that were side-by-side. Cord nudged Alan with his elbow. Alan looked at him, and Cord pointed up. Alan followed his gaze to see some people walking, jogging, and running around a track, high above the gym floor. The floor of the track was clear, made of some sort of high-density glass or plexiglass, Cord thought. There were many wires and sensors embedded all along the track, but you could still see through not only the clear rail that circled the inside of the track for safety, but through the floor of it, watching as shoes padded across. As shoes and naked feet hit the track, lights blinked in the shapes of them. "You should see it with the lights out. It's actually beautiful." Andrea said as she smiled. "Each step taken is recorded by many sensors inside of the track. The track itself is made of a special material - top secret components of course - and the track is mostly solid and inflexible, but is kind of spongy and giving on the surface, so it's not hard on your feet. Kind of like a rubber matt. It has to give on the surface anyway, because of the sensors. You would not believe all of the data that is collected from your feet from a simple stride across the floor!" she said. "It's absolutely amazing." Cord said. "We ain't worgin' out, yed?" Alan said in one of their corny, private languages. "Excuse me?" Andrea asked. "Oh, nothing. I was just inquiring as to when we would be using the facilities." he said, glancing at Cord. "Oh, it'll be a little while yet, before we need you to begin using this equipment." she said. They continued the tour. They noticed that all of the machines had keypads on them, and wires connected to them, going into the floor. Andrea explained in order for the machine to work, you must swipe your keycard for each set you do. This lets the computer know who is on the machine, and it records your workout data. How much weight, how much time between each rep, how much time between each set, et cetera. We can use this data to track your progress and determine the effectiveness of the enhancers, and along with testing your blood work, we can tweak your dosages." she said. "Good grief." Alan said. "What?" Cord asked. "Sounds like a lot of rigmarole." he said. Cord laughed.

"Are all of the people who are here right now a part of the study?" Cord asked. Andrea looked around. "Actually, I don't see anyone from the study here. I'm not the only doctor here. There are several doctors working on a variety of studies and in different stages of the program. I am the doctor for stage I. I handle recruits who are qualified candidates and try to get them through stage I. I've only seen one of my test subjects who made it through stage I, since the program has been going on at this facility . . . for about six months now. Honestly, I guess most people end up quitting the program. Just about everyone working out here, now, are employees taking advantage of the benefit of having a gym." she said. "Why do most people quit?" Alan asked. "I don't know. After they leave me, either by quitting, being released, or advancing to the next stage, I have no further involvement with them, to tell you the truth." she said. "Why would they be released?"

Cord asked. "Well, the enhancers don't work for everyone. If they don't, no one, us or them, is getting any benefit out of the program. Shall we continue our tour?" she finished. "Sure." Alan said.

They walked into the men's locker room area. Andrea did not look the least bit uncomfortable amidst the few guys going about their business in towels. It looked like what you would expect. There was an area with lockers, there was an area with standard toilets and urinals, there were a few sinks with mirrors, and a sauna. Andrea pointed out the best feature to the men. She directed them to a line of eight doors on one wall, across from the locker area. "These, are your private dressing rooms. Each room has a toilet, shower, sink, mirror, and a few cabinets for clothing and personal belongings. Your keycard lets you in. Alan, yours is #4. Cord, yours is #7." she said. They each beeped open their dressing area and looked inside. "Cool." Cord said. "The only thing you have to share in here is the sauna, if you want to take a steam bath." she said. After looking around in the locker room, they exited back out into the main gym area.

Andrea took them into another area of the gym. It was the refreshment area. It looked like a combination lounge and small kitchen. There was a glass door cooler, with many different types of beverages. There was a mixture of diet and regular sodas amongst them. There were cabinets full of everyday food items, such as bread, canned goods, crackers, cereal, and so on. There was a refrigerator loaded with many common food items of the sort that you would see in many homes in America. Very few of them appeared to be healthy snack / meal options. There was the garden variety of kitchen appliances available, including a few that not all standard kitchens would have. There were booths and tables, just like you would see in a restaurant. There was a radio playing softly through a few speakers in the ceiling. There was a juice bar with a variety of protein supplements available. Cord was glad to see the bar, but as he perused the cabinets, the cooler, and the refrigerator, he began to frown. He turned to Doctor Lawson and began to speak, but she beat him to the punch. "I know exactly what you're thinking. Although these amenities are available to anyone with section 2 clearance, you're thinking *Couldn't they have put less junk food in here? Am I right?*" she said. "Well, yeah, pretty much." Cord said. "Well, believe it or not, you don't have to worry about what you eat during the program. At all. You can eat whatever you want. These performance enhancers are revolutionary. Your body will retain whatever is good for it from the food you eat and get rid of the rest as waste. The enhancers will actually be controlling your BMI!" she exclaimed. "Diet companies would go nuts for this stuff." Alan said. "Don't forget the trade secret contracts you signed." Doctor Lawson reminded him, smiling. "I'm no scientist," Cord said "but doesn't the ability for the enhancers to control your BMI go way beyond standard athletic science and maybe even delve into the realm of biophysics and neurophysics?" Alan rolled his eyes. "I can't tell you everything, because some of it, I don't know myself. But, revealing more of what I do know would mean that I was breaking my contract. I wanted to help you understand some, but I may have said too much already. You guys don't want me to get into trouble, do you?" she asked. "No." They both said. "I'm sure there's someone else up the line who can tell you more if you stick around for the duration of the program." she said. "We're just amazed at the whole thing. Cord will try harder to keep his trap shut." Alan said, feigning a serious look.

They had spent nearly two hours in the facility. Andrea explained to them that they no longer needed to be led out, now they had their security badges. They left the facility the same way they came in. Cord went to call Alan while they were in the parking lot. He did not have any service. As they pulled past the gate onto South Boulevard once again, he had service immediately. He called Alan. "Yeah, man." Alan said. "Have you noticed that you don't have *any* service anywhere in the facility. Not even in the parking lot." Cord asked. "Yeah, I did notice. The last time we left, I had fourteen billion voicemails pop up once we left. Can you work out tonight?" Alan said. "Yeah, my wife doesn't care so much with me coming home later from the gym, since we're actually getting paid a little bit of money for this program." Cord answered. Alan laughed and said. "Ten-four. I'll see you there in about 30 minutes."

They both arrived at the fitness center at the same time. Alan, who had changed into his gym clothes in the car, while in transit, walked up to Cord's car. Cord had just finished slipping on his gym shoes. "You ret?" Alan asked. "Yeah, I'm almost ready." said Cord, getting out of his car. "Hey, Alan?" he asked. Alan just raised his eyebrows in response. "Remember when the janitor ran into me and knocked me down?" he asked. Alan smiled and said "How could I forget that? I felt bad for him, but I 'bout lost it over you!" Cord offered a small scrap of paper to Alan. "He stuck this in my hand." Alan looked down at the scrap he was now holding. Although the writing was sloppy, it unmistakably said *please leave this place and don't come back.* Alan looked up at Cord. Neither said a word. No jokes. No comments. Not even any changes in facial expressions. The two men worked out in silence at their local fitness center for a couple of hours before heading home.

Cord walked through his back door and saw his son sitting in his gaming chair in the living room, playing one of his favorite games. Watching his son made him smile from ear to ear. Little Cord looked up. When he saw it was his Dad, his face lit up and he yelled "Dad!" He jumped up from his chair and ran to his Dad, who snatched him up and held him high in the air. Although he was stronger, 70 pounds was still not easy for him to be tossing up. But his son loved it. They hugged and kissed and gave each other "noogies." He could not possibly love anyone more than he loved his little boy. He put him down and Little Cord ran back to his game. Although, a challenging life, he relished the fact that his boy with Down Syndrome would probably always be happy to see him. Cord bent down and kissed his wife, who was sitting on the floor, writing in a composition book. "How'd it go, today?" she asked. "Well, we got to see the gym, but we didn't really get to work out in it." he said. "So, we worked out at ours." He added, forcing a smile. He did not tell her about the note.

Alan's wife met him at the door and they kissed as he walked in. She was holding their little girl, Hayley. "Hey,

Sweetpea!" Alan said as he took her. He held her up over his head and she smiled broadly. He brought her back down to him and she hugged her Daddy around the neck. Alan hugged her and kissed her. Even though he has another child who is a teenager now, it never failed to amaze him that he is actually a father to a tiny human being, who looked up to him and depended on him. He still felt like a kid, himself. He put her down and she sprinted off, heading to a toy with blinking lights and music chirping out of the speaker. He and his wife sat down on the couch. "Hey, honey, have you got to do anything with that study yet?" she asked. "No, not yet. Cord and I are going to just keep doing what we've been doing until someone tells us not to." he said, putting his arm on his wife's shoulders. He had intended on mentioning the note that the janitor had given to Cord to see what his wife thought but decided now was not the right time.

5

Thursday, August 20th

The men were able to let themselves into the facility as far as section 2, now that they had keycards. They reported to Doctor Lawson's office, as she had instructed them the day before. Alan knocked and they heard her say "Come on in." through the door. She was closing a notebook as they walked in. "Okay, guys. Today is the big day." she said. "What's the tour today? Section 3, animal testing?" Cord asked, jokingly. "You're quite the clever one, aren't you?" she asked, rhetorically, as she smiled. "Sorry, Doc, but if you're calling *him* clever, then *you're* not as clever as I thought *you* were." said Alan. They all chuckled. "Sorry, I can neither confirm or deny that hypothesis." she said, smiling again. Doctor Lawson seemed to have high spirits today. This was a welcome change from the feelings both men had from the past few days. "Okay, we'll bite. What is the big day all about?" Cord asked. "You're going to start getting all juiced up." she said.

Both men smiled and nodded their heads, pleased to hear this. "Follow me." she said.

Andrea buzzed them into one of the offices in section 2. A man who appeared to be in his late twenties or early thirties, athletic and ripped, to say the least, good-looking, with dark brown hair styled with hair gel, sat at a computer behind his desk, clicking away on the keyboard. He looked up, smiled, and then stood up. "Hi, Andrea." he said. "Hi, Mark. These are the two I was talking to you about. Alan Carson and Cord Grayson." she said, pointing at each man respectively. "This is Doctor Mark Donovan. He will be administering stage I of the performance enhancers." she said. "Hi, guys. Please, just call me Mark. Andrea, I guess I misunderstood. I know you had told me about both of them, because I have already accessed their files on the network, but I was thinking you were only going to bring them one at a time." he said. "That's okay, Mark. These two special friends can't even be separated with a crowbar." she said, looking at the two men, smiling. They all laughed. "Well, it's no big deal. I've got some time. I can call down to section 6 and have someone meet me in section 3 with a stage I juice starter." she said, reaching for Mark's desk phone. "No, I've got more juice, here. I just need to run to supply and get another syringe." said Doctor Donovan. Andrea's eyes widened. Mark walked over to a safe and swiped his keycard and then punched some numbers into a keypad on the safe. He opened it and retrieved another small vial, identical to the one sitting on his desk. He shut the safe back. He placed the vial next to the other one on his desk with the lone syringe. "Guys, please excuse us for a moment."

said Andrea as she nodded for Mark to walk away from the men across to the other side of his spacious office. Although they were whispering, both men could make out what was being said. "Keeping the juice in your office? Are you nuts?" Andrea asked Mark. "Look, it's a pain in the butt having to get this stuff every time." he said. "Roberson said *Absolutely no serum kept outside of section 6!* If he finds out you're keeping this stuff in your office, it wouldn't surprise me if you got removed from this project . . . or even fired!" she exclaimed in a whisper. "He's not going to find out. I happen to know that we've been using so much of this stuff in testing, they no longer keep track of it by the milliliter." said Mark. "That still doesn't mean he won't find out." Snapped Andrea. "Andrea, are you going to tell him?" Mark asked. Her brows furrowed. "Well, of course not, Mark. You're my friend." She snapped again. "Well, don't worry about it." he said, putting his hand on her shoulder. She shook her head, concerned. She could tell from his physique that he was using the serum for himself and made a mental note to talk to him about it when they could have more privacy. Did he not realize the dangers he could be placing himself into using the juice without proper monitoring? "Look, I won't do it anymore, okay? So relax and don't worry." he said, saying the only thing he could think of to erase the worried look on her face. He could feel the tension subsiding through her shoulder. "Okay." she said. Alan looked at Cord and whispered "I think Mark just got caught with his hand in the cookie jar . . ." They walked back to Cord and Alan. "Let me go get another syringe." Doctor Donovan said. He left the room. "Sorry about that, guys. We just had a little disagreement over policy here at the facility." she said. "Didn't hear a thing." said Cord. Mark returned with a syringe in his hand. "Okay, guys, after Mark gives you your injections, you're free to go. I'll see you two tomorrow, in my office. Mark, I'll talk to you later." she said, stepping through the office doorway. "Okay, Andrea. See you in a bit." he said.

"Okay, guys, drop your pants." said Doctor Donovan. They looked at each other and then proceeded to unbutton their pants. "Whoa, just kidding!" Mark said. "This will be directly into a vein in your arm. Do either of you wish for privacy for the injection?" he asked. Alan said "Don't worry about that – I've seen him cryin' before . . . in fact, a whole lot." Doctor Donovan swabbed their arms with alcohol and gave them their injections. It was a small amount and was over very quickly. "Okay, guys, I know you've already gone over the possible side effects. Something no one may have told you is this: If you experience any of those side effects, call this number." he said, handing them a card that was blank, except for a telephone number. "If the side effects are severe or may even seem life-threatening, you should call this number. Even if you were able to explain to a med tech or a doctor in a hospital your situation, by the time they figured out what to do – if they even could – it would be too late to help you. The team at this number can get to you quicker, and they know what to do. I'm not wanting to scare you, because our new formula rarely has any type of side effects, other than the general ones that you have read about, but this is just a safety measure. Do you have any questions?" Mark finished. Both men shook their heads. "Okay, then. Good luck. I'll let you know when your next injection is." he said, offering his hand to the men. They shook hands all around and then left the office.

The men hadn't spent much time at the facility on this visit, so they were able to get to their local gym closer to what had been their normal time. As they walked in, Alan said "Legs today. It's gonna hurt." Cord mumbled "Daz right." They proceeded to the treadmill, where they did their cardio first. Both men felt great. After an invigorating walk on the machine's maximum incline, they had a sip of water from the fountain, then headed to the Smith machine to do their squats. Cord noticed that although he could not lift any more weight than before, he did not feel as fatigued at the end of their sets. *What could the "miracle juice" do in one day, anyway?* Cord thought. Indeed, by the end of the work out, Alan even said as much. "Man, I don't feel nearly as tired as usual." Cord said "Me neither."

6

Friday, August 21st

Alan called Cord. "Go ahead." Cord said. "Hey, Cord. I'm not going to be coming in today. The baby's sick and my wife can't get off work. I may be able to work out at the gym if my Mother can stay with her. Just call me when you head out." Alan said. "Ten-four. Hope she feels better, soon." said Cord. "Thanks." said Alan. Cord paused before he spoke again. "How do you feel today?" he asked. "I feel pretty good, why?" Alan asked. "I feel *absolutely great.*" Cord said. "Well, yeah, I do, too, I just hate having to take off work, you know." said Alan. "Yeah, I got ya." Cord said. "Okay, I'll talk to you when you head out today." said Alan. "Okay, have a good one." said Cord. "You, too." Alan said. That afternoon, Cord headed down South Boulevard to the facility. He entered as always, and went into Doctor Lawson's office. "Hi, Cord." she said. "Hi." he said. "Where's Alan?" she asked immediately. "His little girl was sick today, and he had to stay home with her." he said. She frowned and looked down at her desk, beginning to softly chew on the bottom of her lip, as if in deep thought. She looked back up at him. "Cord, you guys have got to be here, every day, five days a week. You did sign a contract, remember?" she said, firmly. "Uh, excuse me *Doctor Lawson,*" Cord began, "but you must not have heard what I said: His little girl is sick." he said firmly. "I heard you and I understand that. But this program is top priority." she said with conviction. Cord was sure that his entire bald head had turned red and was about to explode. "Well, I'm here to tell you right now, don't nothin' come before my son . . . and I know I'm going out on a limb here, but I'm darn sure Alan feels the same way about his daughter." Cord snapped. Doctor Lawson drew in a deep breath and then blew it out. "I'm not saying that. If we need to make arrangements for his wife to be home with his child, and even compensate for missed income, then we will do so. But, you guys . . . must . . . be . . . *here.*" she said, pronouncing each word aggressively. Cord remained quiet, still very much irritated. "Follow me." she said as she stood up from her desk. She led him to the *Primary Care* office. Doctor Kitridge was sitting at his desk doing paperwork. "Hi, Doctor Kitridge. Could you please take a blood sample from Cord. This will be for the first day after the stage I juice starter. I also need a kit and a cold pack where I can take a sample out in the field." she said. "I presume that will be for Alan." said Doctor Kitridge. "Yes." she said. "You know . . ." Doctor Kitridge began. "I know Roberson doesn't like it, but these circumstances are beyond my control. I'll bring the sample straight back here, tonight. You aren't going to rat me out, are you Doctor?" she asked.

"Oh, no. I don't like Roberson any more than you do. I just want the seas to remain calm." said Doctor Kitridge, as he pushed the needle into Cord's vein. "Okay, I can't leave the facility until about 5:30 pm. If you talk to Alan before then, tell him to expect a call from me around that time. I have to meet him somewhere to take a blood sample." she said. "I will. Look, I'm sorry this has caused so much trouble . . . but it's the man's kid, for cryin' out loud." Cord said. "I know. I know that your children come first. But, this project is very sensitive. Unless it's an absolute emergency, you guys have to be here every day, even if it's just briefly for a sample or an injection. If something unexpected like this comes up, call me, just like you would call your employer, so we can make other arrangements. You guys did read those contracts you signed, right?" Andrea asked, smiling sarcastically. "I'll see *you* Monday. Have a good weekend." She added. "You, too, Andrea." Cord said only half-heartedly as he reached for his phone. He was going to call Alan immediately but remembered he had to check his phone with the guard. Not that it would have worked inside of the facility anyway.

As he pulled onto South Boulevard, he called Alan to let him know what was going on. After he finished telling him, Alan said "Forget those clowns. When my kid needs me, I'm gonna be there." Cord said "I know and that's what I told Doctor Lawson." Alan said "Well, if this crap gets out of hand, then I guess I'll just have to quit. I'll see you at the gym about 4:30." Cord agreed.

Alan was already on the treadmill when Cord walked into the gym. He stepped up onto one of the empty treadmills beside Alan, put his audio player on, placed his keys and phone on the machine, and then ramped the machine up to the maximum incline setting, just as Alan had his machine set. Alan, being much taller than Cord, had a greater stride. He almost always had the treadmill on the maximum incline, a setting of 15, walking at a steady pace. Cord would usually start off that way and then switch it up between walking, running, and jogging, as he adjusted the incline for what his body could handle without becoming over-fatigued. Cord had noticed that although Alan was still walking, his machine was set on a higher rate of speed than what he was used to seeing. He quickly felt the necessity to increase his machine's speed with his faster gait as well. Whereas normally, he would give his heart and body some time to adjust to the initial strain of this cardiovascular exercise, he didn't seem to be experiencing that resistance or the occurrence of a second wind to begin his jogging. He cranked the machine up to 5.5 and reduced the incline to 6 and began jogging. He still experienced no resistance whatsoever. He wasn't even winded. He looked over at Alan, who was walking steadily with his large stride. He had a big, goofy grin on his face and was staring at one of the plasma TV screens, watching some silly TV show, without any headphones for sound. Cord looked back at the controls on his own treadmill. He ran the machine up to 6.5 and increased his jog to a sprint, waiting for the slightly labored breathing to start. *This is crazy.* Cord thought to himself. He punched in 8 on the speed and matched the pace of the treadmill. He looked over at Alan, who still had not paid him any attention. He pushed the incline up, steadily, until he was back at 15, the machine's maximum. He was running on the treadmill as fast as he thought he could, at the maximum incline setting. He could feel the resistance of climbing a hill, but with no exhausting effects. He wasn't sweating. He wasn't breathing hard. He wasn't even really trying all that hard! He pulled the earphones out of his ears and switched off his MP3 player. He looked over at Alan, once again, this time saying his name loudly. Alan turned his gaze from the TV to his friend. Alan saw Cord's legs scissoring faster than he had ever seen them move. He looked at his face and saw Cord's eyes were wide and questioning. Even though his legs were flying, he was able to have his torso partly turned toward Alan with his arms halfway up and hands opened as if saying *What the heck?* Cord shook his head with alarm and hit the stop button on the treadmill, and hopped off before it had barely slowed down. He walked quickly down the aisle, then out the front entrance. Several gym employees said "'Bye." He didn't pay them any attention. Alan had stopped his machine and followed Cord.

Alan found Cord outside, pacing back and forth in front of a decorative planter by the front entrance. He appeared to be talking as he paced. As he got within earshot, he could hear him. " . . . I'm not hallucinating, I'm pretty sure I'm not dead, I'm definitely not asleep . . ." he was saying to himself. "What the heck was that all about?" Alan asked, interrupting Cord's one-man conversation. Cord stopped pacing and looked at Alan. "I don't know. It's got to be . . ." Cord looked around and saw a couple of gym members walking by them toward the entrance. He stepped closer to Alan and dropped his voice to a whisper. "It's got to be the effects of the enhancer. Did you see how fast I was going on an incline of 15? But it's only been, what, two days?" he finished. "We just got the injections yesterday." Alan said rather loudly. "Shhh!" Cord said in a whisper. "Nobody knows what the crap we're talking about." Alan said. "I want to keep it that way, remember that darn contract we signed . . ." Cord said. "Screw that thing." said Alan. Cord walked a little further down beside the planter, away from the entrance to the gym. "Did you not notice anything?" Cord asked. "Well, I'm so used to walking that steady pace on the incline, It's honestly not really that hard for me, anyway. I did crank up the pace a little because it did seem a little easier than usual." He answered. Cord looked down and nodded in thought. "Hey, this is a good thing. A bit more than what I was expecting, but a good thing, right? Let's go finish our workout and don't worry about a *good* thing." Alan said.

The two walked back into the gym, heading to the water fountain for a quick drink. Alan's phone rang and he answered it. It was Doctor Lawson. She said she was heading to Gastonia to meet him to get a blood sample. He gave her the name of the restaurant on the corner, near the gym as their meeting place, because you could not really see the gym well from the road. They agreed to meet in about 45 minutes.

Their first exercise was dips. They had weight assistance to start with, but both men took them off on their second set. They both breezed through the dips without even a strain. They both noticed that they had a few people watch them, seemingly impressed with the speed and effortlessness that they went through the exercise. Neither man was really thirsty, but they went to the water fountain out of habit and to keep themselves hydrated. "Okay, now I see what you mean." Alan said. They headed over to the free weight area and stopped in front of the dumbbells. Cord grabbed a 50-pounder and Alan grabbed a 75-pounder, which was the heaviest dumbbell available in the gym. Both men raised the dumbbell over their heads, and then lowered it behind their heads, holding it by one end. They then began lowering it and raising it behind their backs. Although, they could feel the pressure and resistance of their bodies working and in motion, there was no straining and grunting. In fact, each man was feeling only what they could describe as a "rush." Their pulses quickened, their bodies tightened, and their breathing got heavier, but all without any negative or uncomfortable side effects. On top of that, even their minds were affected in a positive manner. They could think more clearly, although it felt as if they were being flooded with endorphins. The feeling was borderline euphoric. For this exercise, however, it seemed as if there was very little effort. When they quickly finished a set of ten, they looked at each other in amazement. Cord racked the 50-pounder and pulled the other 75-pounder. They breezed through another set. Cord was surprised to find that he seemed to handle the heavier weight just as easily as the 50-pounder he had just racked. "I feel like I'm wasting my time." Alan said as they racked the 75-pounders, not even doing a third set. "I know this isn't a part of our *Arm Workout*, but I want to try something . . ." he added, hurrying to the free weights at the weight bench.Andrea pulled up to the rear of the restaurant, so as to have a little privacy when she took Alan's blood sample. She glanced up to look at the clock on her dashboard. She had made very good time on the interstate, but it looked as though she was going to have to wait another fifteen minutes or so for Alan. As she looked around, she noticed that there were several stores in the shopping center, behind the restaurant. She also noticed the gym at the end of the building. Something seemed awfully familiar about that place. She thought about it for a little while until, suddenly, it dawned on her. That was the sticker Alan had on the rear window of his car, the name of that gym. *No, surely he's not working out in a public facility.* She thought. She had told them they did not need to work out. *Need. She had said "need."* She had not given them explicit instructions to not work out. Why was she so worried? A young child could probably understand the necessity to keep every aspect of the study confidential and out of public view. Not to mention all of the paperwork that they had read and signed, explaining this to them. She quickly shifted her car back into drive and headed over to the fitness center.

They loaded a barbell up with the heaviest weight Alan had most recently lifted. He lay down on the bench. Cord took the spotter's position. He went through ten reps as if he was pumping helium balloons instead of iron. He racked it back easily. He just tilted his head back, and looked at Cord, upside down, with a smile spreading across his face, and said *"That* has never been easier." Cord was looking down at him. "My turn." he said, grinning. Cord took his place on the bench, and Alan spotted him. Out of habit, Alan assisted

Cord in getting the barbell off of the rack. As he watched Cord fly through ten reps in utter Amazement, he knew that the assistance had not been necessary. Cord was still holding the barbell up in the air on his last rep, when he said quietly to Alan "Alan, watch this." He easily scooted both hands toward the center of the bar. He took a deep breath, then removed one hand. He felt gentle swellings in his arms and chest muscles. That same rush and borderline euphoric feeling engulfed him, and he felt as if his muscles were actually growing and strengthening on demand. He was holding 225 pounds up with one hand! He did ten, quick, one-handed reps and then racked the barbell. Alan quickly looked around and saw that no one had been paying them any attention. *As usual.* He thought. Cord jumped up from the bench. They both were smiling at each other. They gave each other a discreet "five." When they laughed about it later, both of them agreed that they almost gave each other a hug. Both of them actually had tears forming in their eyes with a strange joy that neither man could really understand at the time. They loaded two more plates on each side, bringing the total up to 405 pounds. Cord looked around the free weight area. Everyone was still absorbed in their own weight training, and still, no one was paying them any attention. Alan lay down on the bench. He rubbed his hands together slowly, and then placed them on the barbell, preparing to attempt to lift it from the rack. Cord was in the spotter's position once again. "Don't . . . do it." said a firm, female voice as Andrea stepped up behind Alan, next to Cord. She had a furious look on her face, looking back and forth between the two men. Alan tilted his head back and saw her angry face upside-down. The look she was giving them could have burned a hole through all of the steel plates on the bar. He slowly lowered his hands and arms down to his side.

Andrea and the two men were congregated next to her large SUV. She began taking Alan's blood sample. "I can't believe you two." she said, jamming the needle in Alan's arm. "Ow!" he exclaimed, automatically, even though he barely felt anything. She looked at him through narrow eyes. "I know you didn't feel that." she said harshly. "Look, Andrea . . ." Cord began. "No. Just stop right there. I don't even want to hear it. I want you two in my office first thing after work on Monday. I don't want you two clowns in public view from now until then, even if it means starving to death over the weekend, understand?" she said, hotly. The two men both nodded, but remained silent as she finished up her sampling and packed the samples away in the small cooler. Cord could see in Alan's eyes that he had had just about enough. Cord knew that Alan was holding back because he was so giddy from the potential gains he could make from the program. She slammed the driver's door as she got back into her car. She pulled away, not saying another word to them, or even looking at them. "Oops. I guess we really screwed up." said Cord. "Nobody saw anything. I'm not going to put up with this malarkey." Alan said. Cord nodded and said "I know, but that doesn't seem to matter to her. Look, just give it another chance. Let's see what she has to say on Monday." They stood in silence a little longer, then Alan said "Well, I'll think about it. I'll call you Monday morning. Have a good weekend." Cord said "You, too. Hope Hayley gets better soon." The two men left the fitness center.

7

Monday, August 24th

After work, the two men met in Andrea's office with her as she had instructed them. They exchanged pleasantries, but there was still some tension in the air. "Okay," she began. "Here are copies of your contracts." she said as she plopped their contracts down on her desk, in front of each man. She made no effort to set them down gently. "Did you read these before you signed them?" she asked. Both men nodded. "Mostly." Cord said. "Okay, well I'd like for you to read them again if you are unsure about their contents. I am, however, going to stress some of the subject matter." she said. Andrea had a copy of the contract, and leafed through it quickly, before stopping. "It says:" she began. *"Study participant may not perform, exhibit, display, or otherwise reveal said participant's enhanced capabilities by way of visuals, documentation, verbal, or any other means to anyone not clearly identified as a member of the staff within the study team. Enhanced capabilities are defined as exceeding the typical and/or normal capabilities of the participant as of the last date before the study began."* In other words, what you can do as a result of the performance enhancers is to be kept secret." she said. "I can't believe you two did not know any better, even if you had not read *any* of the contract." she added. "I guess we really didn't believe that the results we would achieve would be of any real significance." Alan said. "You know, I'll buy that. But, when you realized that this was the real deal, why didn't you stop your little show Friday?" she asked. They both looked down, guiltily. "Just excited, I guess." Cord said. "Ok, *boys,* we have now established that what we're doing here *ain't no joke.* We can still have fun and games, but not in public, alright? And Alan, I understand about your little girl. Of course, you're going to put her first. Just make arrangements, okay?" she said. Both men nodded. They were walking to the gym with Andrea by their side when Cord asked "What exactly are the enhancers doing to us?" Andrea swiped her card at the Section 2 entrance, and they walked through. "I believe I have explained everything about the enhancers that I am authorized to. You may be able to find out some more from Doctor Donovan, when you see him again." They walked into the gym. "But, for now, this is Tracie Barrett. I guess you could say that she will be your personal trainer." They shook hands all around. Tracie was a petite woman, wearing slacks and a silk shirt. She was very professional looking with her thick-rimmed glasses, holding a tablet PC. She was pretty, but she looked more like a librarian than a personal trainer. "Well, with the enhancers in your system, there won't really be a lot of training involved, but we will do a lot of monitoring and testing to record and track your performance increases. I will mostly be around just to watch and assist you if you have any questions about how to operate any of the equipment. I will also be asking you questions about how you feel and direct you to use certain machines or run the track periodically." she said. "What do they need to do this afternoon?" asked Andrea. "Well, today, I want them just to explore the equipment and do whatever they want to do with it. I'll be here, monitoring their performance." she said, patting the tablet PC she was holding ". . . and answering any questions." she finished. "Very good." said Andrea, looking at the two men. "Well, spend as much time as you want, but come by my office before you leave." she added as she raised her hand for goodbye. The three waved back and Andrea turned and left the gym. "Okay, guys, I've got a little office in the corner." she said, pointing to one corner of the gym. "If you need me, and don't see me walking around, check in my office. Have a good time." she said as she turned to walk away. "Thanks." Both men chimed at the same time. "You're welcome." she said.

Today, the gym was empty, except for the two men and Tracie. After they had changed into their gym clothes, they took turns picking different machines to test their new-found strength. They each had to swipe their keycard for their turn on the machine. Alan finally got to bench the 405 pounds he did not get to try the previous Friday, but there was no one around to be impressed, but Cord, who was able to do it as well. Tracie walked up, as Cord finished his last set on the bench press. "Oh, yeah, guys, by the way – let's not do any weightlifting over about 500 pounds right now. Your bodies are actually physically able to, and you would still feel fine right now, but the strain on them is tremendous, and the damage you could do to yourselves could be severe. We need to do more testing and tweaking with the formula to find the right balance of maximum, but safe, effectiveness of the enhancers, ok?" she said. "Ok." said Alan. "Miss Barrett?" Cord said. "Yes?" she answered. "Can you tell us anything about how the enhancers work?" he asked. "Anything Andrea has told you is probably a lot more than I know. Around here, it seems like information concerning the enhancers is given out strictly on a need-to-know basis, even amongst the staff. Not that I would understand how it works, anyway." she said. "Okay, thanks anyway." he said. She smiled and walked away, studying the screen on her tablet PC. Cord looked at Alan. "I want to know how this stuff works and what it's doing to us." he said. "Who cares?" Alan asked. As Cord sighed, Alan added "Nahh, I'm just kidding, banana head, but I am willing to deal with some side effects for the benefits we're getting. 500 pounds with little effort, and that's just the beginning! Just think, it wasn't long ago that I was talking junk to you for another one of your hair-brained schemes. You *really* hooked us up this time, Cord." Cord was silent. Alan did have a point. This setup could not be any more perfect. It seems like overnight, he had noticed that he and Alan both had developed thicker, more impressive curves of muscles in all the right places. He even noticed his "problem area" – the little area of fat that he still had on his stomach – was shrinking. "Yeah, I guess so." Cord said. He still couldn't shake the feeling that things were still going just a bit *too* well. And of course, he being who he is, just wanted to know *everything*. "You ready to get the heck out of here?" Alan asked. "Yeah, let's go."

They had not really worked up a sweat. Both men went to the locker room to change and use the restroom. They stopped by Tracie's office, where she was steadily punching keys on a computer. "'Bye, Miss Barrett." Alan said. "'Bye." said Cord. She looked up from the computer. "Guys, call me Tracie. I'll see you tomorrow. Have a good evening." she said. "You, too." they said. They headed out into the hallway. As the door closed behind them, Cord caught sight of a familiar face. The janitor was just swiping his card to go into section 3. "Hey, Joe!" Cord said in a loud whisper. Joe looked up, startled, and made eye contact with Cord. He then looked around and saw that the hallway was clear, except for the three of them. He motioned for the men to approach. "Go on to Andrea's office. Tell her that I had to take a dump or something. I'll catch up." Cord said to Alan. "Ten-four." Alan said. Cord walked quickly toward Joe, as Alan headed down the hallway in the other direction. Joe looked through the large door into section 3, back and forth, then motioned for Cord to follow him. Joe quickly led Cord into one of the office doorways labeled *Sanitation.*

The room, although small, was filled with all kinds of janitorial goodies. Some of them appeared to be hi-tech. There were shelves filled with disinfectants, spill absorbers, packages of paper towels, garbage bags, assorted cleaners, brushes, and the like. There was a small locker on one wall, and a small card table against the opposite wall. There was a small TV, an ashtray, and an opened pack of potato chips on the table.

There was a single chair at the table, but there were two stacked boxes of toilet tissue on one side of the table, adjacent to the other chair, obviously serving as chair #2. *For when Joe entertains guests.* Cord thought and smiled. "You like my little setup, do ya?" the old, black man asked as he saw the smile on Cord's face. "Oh, yes sir. You got it going on." Cord said. "Have a seat." Joe said, as he eased himself into the chair. Cord hopped on the boxes of tissue. "Where you from?" Joe asked. "Kings Mountain. How 'bout you?" Cord responded. "Been in Charlotte my whole life." Joe said. Cord nodded. "Got a family?" Joe asked. "Yeah, I got a wife and 10-year-old son. Got a step-daughter living on her own." he said. "What about you, Joe?" he asked. "Me? No, I ain't got nobody. I'm 76 years old. My only kid died 15 years ago. Lost my wife about 10 years ago. I got a few relatives scattered 'round about, out-of-state. Don't never see 'em anymore." he said. They were both quiet for a few moments.

Alan quietly walked into Doctor Lawson's office and sat down in front of her desk. She had her back turned to him and was shuffling through a file cabinet. He spied a candy dish and helped himself to a piece. When he opened the candy, the rustling sound of the cellophane made Andrea jump, and she turned to him quickly. "Oh, you startled me. Where's Cord?" she asked. "Nature was calling and he led me to believe it would be wanting him for a while." he said, smiling. She returned his smile. "Well, we can wait for him to get here, before we go over a few things I wanted to discuss. How did your workout go?" she asked. "It went great. This is just absolutely unbelievable. I never imagined *these* results and in such little time." he said. "Just think, if all goes well, this may only be the beginning." she said. "It just doesn't seem like it could get any better. What do you mean by *if all goes well?*" he asked. "There are the side effects we discussed, of course. We're going to do everything possible to keep those at bay. You can't expect your body to do these absolutely amazing feats with no repercussions. With you being from the old school of weight training, I'm sure you're more familiar with the real meaning of the phrase *No Pain, No Gain* than most people. Part of your success will boil down to how bad you want this, and how much pain you are willing to endure to have it. I don't necessarily mean pain as in physical pain, although there will most likely be some of that, too." she said, smiling. "Well, I've wanted this for a long time. I intend to stick with the program." Alan said. "That's good to hear. How about Cord?" she asked. "Well, he can be a real trooper when he wants to be, but he tends to over-analyze everything." he said. "That's not always a bad thing, is it?" she said. "No, I don't guess it is, always." he said.

After a few moments, Cord broke the silence between Joe and himself. "Well, Joe, I know we're not just here to talk about our lives, although I do enjoy it . . ." he began. "We might be doin' *just* that." Joe interrupted. "What do you mean?" asked Cord. "Talkin' 'bout our lives. Look, son . . . this ain't no place for you boys to be hanging out. It's dangerous. You wouldn't believe some of the crap goin' on in here. I'm tellin' ya the truth. I've seen so many come and go and never see 'em again, it ain't even funny." Joe said with a solemn look about him. "Why *would* you see them again, if they have completed the study?" Cord asked. "Look, I *know*. They've had other folks in here, young and old, participatin' in that *study* as you call it. Seems like everything's going along just fine, then all of the sudden, they're gone. And look here – they got animals down in here that they shootin' full of some mess - some of it I know is like what they givin' y'all. How many of them you think have *completed* their *study?"* he asked. Before Cord could speak, he began again. "Not a darn one, that's how many! I've had to clean up some of the messes left over from those poor critters." He finished. "Well, if you feel that strongly about it, then maybe we should have the police look into it . . ." Cord started. "Crap, boy! This here is the federal government! These suckers do whatever the heck they want! Look, we'd better let you get going before Doctor Lawson starts lookin' for you." he said. "I'd like to talk more with you, if I can." Cord said. "We will. We'll talk more. I'm telling you, though - you'd better be figurin' on gettin' out of this mess before you boys get in any deeper." Joe said. He made sure the coast was clear, then hurried Cord back through the section 3 doorway.

Andrea glanced at her watch and then stood up. "I think we need to go check on Cord, huh? He could be having a reaction to the enhancer." she said. "Oh, you don't know Cord. There could be a reaction alright, but it probably most likely resembles a *nuclear reaction.* He might be in there forever." Alan said. "Well, let's just go make sure." she said as she walked toward the office door. Alan began to stand up when her office door swung open and Cord stepped through. "Sorry to keep you waiting." he said to Andrea. "Boy, Cord

. . . that must have been a monster." Alan said. "Yeah, but now, I feel like a million bucks." Cord said, smiling. Andrea motioned for him to sit in the chair next to Alan, and then she sat back down behind her desk. "Well, Cord, Alan and I have already discussed a little bit about your workout, and he seems to think everything went okay. Do you feel the same way, Cord?" she asked. "Yes, I look and feel great. I have not had any ill effects from the enhancer so far." he said. "Well, that's good news. If you were going to have any of the nastier side effects, as our prior studies have shown us, you would most likely have already had them. You guys have had the very latest, updated batches that were tested, tweaked, and re-tweaked to be the finest enhancers yet. You *will,* no doubt, surely have *some* negative effects sometime during the course of this study, but hopefully, those will be mild. *But,* the windows of opportunities for the major effects have most likely closed." she said. "Such as?" Cord asked. She began listing some of them for the men. "Well, death, of course, was always a possibility. I would call that major, wouldn't you? Let's see, there was the chance of violent seizures with your body's rejection of the enhancer, there was the chance of your muscles bursting from an imbalance caused by the improper ratio of the enhancer with your body's chemistry, there, of course, is liver failure from the overproduction of . . ." Cord interrupted. "Okay, okay, we got it. *NOW* you tell us." he said. "All of this information . . ." she began. "Is in our contracts." Alan finished. She gave Alan the thumbs-up. "Has anyone ever died from this, Doctor Lawson?" he asked. Her eyes widened from his question. "I am not aware of anyone dying from the use of the enhancers, although there is always that possibility. I'm fairly new in the program, but from what I've heard, the formula has come a long way over the years and it's the best ever. I've seen some very positive results, and you two have come at the right time to participate in what could be the history-making version of this formula. This brings us to the major point I was wanting to discuss with you guys. You've had a taste of what you can do from the initial stage I enhancer. You could stop now, and over a few weeks, the enhancer will gradually be out of your system. Your body will feel like it's been hit by a freight train and you will have a wicked headache during this period. We, of course, will give you medication to alleviate the pain as much as possible. And you'll be back to normal as if you'd never even taken it to begin with. *Or -* you could take a leave of absence from your employer, and make the study your primary employment for the time being. From my understanding, the enhancers themselves are basically preparing your body for the adjustment of a more permanent condition, if you are able to tolerate the process to get through to the end of the program. You would actually be living here at the facility, but you would be getting paid for that, too. We, of course, would handle everything, and your regular jobs would be waiting on you, once the program was completed. But, who knows, you may end up finding an interest here, and staying on in some capacity, after the study is over. There are several employees in various places connected to the program that did just that. Unfortunately, they did not get to achieve our desired results, but they liked what we were doing and they were happy to be placed to continue to help in the program." she said. Without delay, Alan said "Count me in!" Cord still had the conversation with Joe floating around in his head. *This is a study funded by the federal government. They wouldn't do anything to jeopardize the safety of their citizens, right? Bullcrap.* Cord's thoughts were crowding his mind as Alan and Doctor Lawson looked at him, waiting for his response. "Can I think about it?" he asked. "What the heck is there to think about? Working out all the time. Giving us a break from having to deal with contractors and property owners. No paperwork. It'll be like a paid vacation!" Alan exclaimed, with a mildly irritated look on his face. Andrea came to Cord's rescue. "You can take a month to think about it. Both of your profiles have worked out perfectly for the program. But, by the end of next month, I will need to hand you off to begin stage II trials. Let me know something by . . . the morning of Friday, September 25th at the latest." she said, thumbing through the calendar on her desk. "If you can't tell me *yes* by then, as much as I'd hate to see you go, I'd have to drop you from the study." she said. "I will. I'll think about it and let you know." he said. Alan was shaking his head slowly.

On their way home, Cord called Alan. "Pull over at the exit you take to go home, I need to talk to you." Cord said. "Good grief." Alan said. When they left interstate 85, and pulled up the ramp, both men pulled over onto the shoulder. Cord got out and went back to Alan's car, where Alan was emptying his passenger seat of work papers, clearing it for Cord to sit down. "What now, cry-baby?" Alan asked. "Alan, the janitor, told me that there were all kinds of crazy stuff going on in the facility. He said they were experimenting on animals with awful results. Participants in the study would be there for a short time, and then suddenly be gone." Cord said. "Look, Cord, I know how you are - instead of just taking an apparently good thing, you're the type of person who has to size it up, look it over, evaluate it, and study it. There's nothing wrong with that. I like that about you. But, some- times, you miss things in life because you take too much time thinking them over, and the next thing you know, the oppor- tunity's gone. Maybe the janitor's not a nutty old codger. Maybe he is. But, come on. This is a clinical study funded by the government. Yeah, they probably have had the animals doped up with different experiments . . . maybe even the same stuff they're giving us. They might be pumping them so full of the stuff that it's blowing their brains out or something. But, don't you think that if they had been bringing people in for the study, and the people kept getting sick or dying and disappearing, someone would have noticed by now? Families and friends? I'm sure the government does a lot of monkey business, but I just don't think this is it. I think we both lucked up and got in on something fantastic just in the nick of time. I don't want to blow this opportunity . . . and I don't want you to blow it for yourself, either. But, you are the only one that can make that decision." Alan said. Cord was quiet, letting everything Alan said sink in. "But, why would Joe be telling us these things and trying to warn us? What reason would he have for making anything up?" Cord asked. "Who says he's making it up? He may have seen some bad results from some of the animal testing. You heard what Doctor

Lawson said could have happened to us with the side effects. I'm sure they take more risks and push the animals harder than they do the people. As for people disappearing - well, if you say *no* about continuing with the study, he'll see you disappear after the end of September, right? I'm sure people are coming and going all of the time." Alan said. Cord was quiet. Alan did have a point. "Maybe you're right . . ." Cord said solemnly. "Cord, we'll still keep an open mind. If things begin to seem like they're not quite right come the deadline, we'll quit. It's that simple." Alan said. Cord nodded slowly.

Neither man had any problems convincing their spouses and families that this would be a good thing. Even though Andrea had been unable to give them a definitive duration of the study, except that it would not last for more than a year, there was no doubt that tripling their salary for any length of time was going to make anyone complain. She had also assured them that their families would be able to visit with them at the facility on some weekends. She also made it abundantly clear that they would not be able to leave the facility for any reason without prior approval and accompaniment by authorized personnel for obvious security reasons.

During the course of the month, Alan and Cord enjoyed their workouts at the facility. They gave their blood samples and took their injections. They took advantage of all that the facility had to offer. They both had really grown fond of Tracie Barrett, their personal trainer. Although the enhancers were keeping their performance at such a level that their form during their workouts played a very small role, she was still able to give them pointers from time-to-time that both men thought were very helpful. She constantly reminded them to keep their lifting limited to around 500 pounds, or the results to their bodies could be devastating if something went wrong with the enhancers at this point. They did not push their luck. They also saw Joe from time-to-time, heading down one hallway or another, or into one office or another, pulling a rolling mop bucket or rolling a waste can, but he always seemed to be in a hurry to get to where he was going. Once, Cord had made eye contact with him and made a move to approach him. Joe quickly broke the gaze and moved hurriedly on his way to whatever sanitation disaster may have awaited him. Cord frowned. Things were going so well for him and Alan, the talk he had with that crazy, old janitor began to seem like a distant memory.

8 |

Thursday, September 24th

Although Alan appreciated what the enhancers were doing for him, he didn't much care how they worked. He, of course, was amazed, but was mostly concerned with how he could squeeze the most performance out of them. Cord, on the other hand, although equally amazed, was also intrigued by what could only be super-advanced, mind-numbing science to do what the enhancers were capable of doing. He was constantly trying to pry information about the science behind the enhancers, and how they worked from the various personnel that he and Alan came in contact with.

Tracie knew very little about how the enhancers worked, but she had a good understanding of what the human body could do while using them. Andrea had told them a few general things about how they worked, but clammed up and said that was all she could tell them. He felt she knew a great deal more than what she was sharing with them, but he was not convinced that she knew enough to satiate his thirst for answers to what exactly the enhancers were doing to their bodies and how they did it. There was one constant in his various prying, however, and that was Doctor Donovan. Tracie and Andrea both had surely grown weary of Cord's continual questions and they both referred him to Doctor Donovan. He had, therefore, focused most of his inquisitive efforts on the good doctor. Mark Donovan usually rewarded him with the same general information that Andrea had already given him. He also threw in a few scientific words here and there that Cord couldn't really understand, anyway. Upon using an internet search engine at home to research some of the words he remembered Mark using, he was given another barrage of scientific words that he had heard of before, but could not really understand. *Proteins, adrenaline, adenosine triphosphate, etc.* Upon looking up these new words, he would get some other new words. As he looked those up, he eventually began looping back around to some of the terms he had started with. Although, there was insightful information from his reading of the various definitions and articles with a general understanding of how the human body worked and interacted with some of these various terms, unsurprisingly, they held nothing that really enlightened him on how some sort of interaction with these functions could enhance and increase the body's abilities and performance. After all, the *how* was the trick, wasn't it?

Today, however - as far as his information gathering was concerned - was Cord's lucky day. For whatever reasons he may have had, Mark decided to loosen up on some of the big secrets. Alan rolled his sleeve down after receiving his injection from Doctor Donovan. "Cord, I'm gonna go ahead and head to the fitness center. I gotta take a big dump." Alan said, smiling. "Ugh." Cord said frowning, as he rolled up his sleeve for his injection. Doctor Donovan, who was getting the hypo ready, said "Not to worry. This facility has high velocity fans built into the duct-work, tied into the biosensors. Upon the detection of poisonous gases, they will kick on automatically." Cord and Alan both chuckled. Doctor Donovan smiled. "Nothing can stop this." Alan said in a superhero voice as he walked out of the office. Mark swabbed Cord's injection site with alcohol, then gave him his dose of enhancer. "You two are something else." Doctor Donovan said. "Yeah, we're real conversation pieces, alright." Cord said. "Okay, you're all done." Doctor Donovan said, as he disposed of the needle in the red container on the wall. "How do you know how much to give us each time? I've noticed that the dosage isn't always the same, but it's not always an increase, either." Cord said, pulling his sleeve back down. "You are very observant. And persistent." Mark said. "Hey, I gotta be me." Cord said. "Okay . . . you've worn me down. I'm gonna let loose of a little information that could get me in big trouble." he said. "I've seen where you tend to bend the rules from time-to-time." Cord said, smiling. "I'll tell you what, after your workout, drop back by the office before you leave the facility and I'll explain everything I know about how your body works, and how the enhancers supplement it." said Mark. After their workout, Cord told Alan that he was staying behind for a few minutes to talk to Doctor Donovan. Alan laughed at the thoughts of Cord's constant prying for information. Cord grinned. They waved as Alan walked through the door, heading home.

Mark Donovan walked over to a small 3' x 2' dry erase board on the wall, opposite his desk, next to the door to his office. It had a few indiscernible notes, a couple of calendar dates, and a scraggly picture of a hanging man with x's for the eyes scribbled on it. Memories of high school fluttered back in Cord's mind as Mark picked up the eraser and began wiping away the multi-colored notes. Wearing his white doctor's overcoat, he could have easily passed for a biology teacher getting ready to share notes on the reproduction system of an earthworm with his class. Cord would find that this lesson plan was going to be a bit more complex. Mark drew a rough outline of the human body in the center of the board, with the black marker. "Uh, if that's me, Doc, you forgot the privates." Cord said, jokingly. Doctor Donovan picked the black marker back up and placed a small dot between the sketch's legs. He looked back at Cord, with his eyebrows raised, smiling. "Better?" he asked. Cord simply nodded. He had brought that one on himself. He then used blue and traced around the inside of the sketch. "These represent your blood vessels." With red, he drew some ovals down each upper arm, lower arm, upper leg, and lower leg areas. "These will represent your muscles." He picked up purple and drew the sketch of a brain. He used yellow for a rough representation along the outline of the sketch for the nervous system. "Okay, this is you." he said, using the closed marker in his hand to tap the sketch on the board. "Whenever you want to do anything with your body, your brain sends the signals to the right place via your nervous system. Let's keep it simple and say you were going to lift a glass of water from the table. The brain signals . . ." He used the closed marker and moved it across the sketch on the board from the brain down the yellow line, along the length of one arm, to the end in the hand, as he continued speaking. ". . . for your arm to make the movements necessary to move toward the glass, and then sends the signals necessary for your hand to grasp the glass, so on and so forth. This is done in a fraction of a second. You may have thought to yourself *I want to pick up that glass of water,* but you didn't actively think the commands to make your arm and hand do that, right? Of course not. Well, along with that automatic response from your limb, your limb is sending signals back to your brain. *Okay, brain, I need X amount of blood flow to power my deltoid, my tricep, my bicep, my brachioradialis, and my extensor and flexor muscles.* Your fingers actually have no muscles. The bones in them are pulled by the muscles in your forearm. Well, the brain takes the data provided by the limb through your nervous system and analyzes it. The brain then sends the necessary signals to make it happen. *Lungs, suck in X amount of air as needed. Heart, please increase to X beats per minute to accommodate X amount of oxygen in my blood if necessary.* Of course, the nerve cells are what tell the muscles to contract and do their stuff. You've got two types of protein, *Actin,* and *Myosin,* that turn energy into motion. ATP, or *Adenosine Triphosphate,* an energy molecule, powers these two proteins. Most cells in the human body are tiny, but muscle cells span the entire length of the muscle and can be over a foot long. It can take trillions of myosin heads and billions of actin filaments to move one muscle. What a coordination job, huh? Well, that's just for a simple task, nothing of the magnitude of the kind of performance we are looking for here in the study." Doctor Donovan said. He walked over to his desk and picked up a bottle of water, and took a sip, and then continued. "Your body has a few different ways to come up with energy to power your muscles. The standard method is *Aerobic Metabolism.* This is simply when you are getting a sufficient supply of oxygen to your blood to support your level of activity. For example, if you were walking at a brisk pace and you were breathing in and out sufficiently to provide the volume of oxygen your body needed, your heart was beating effectively and circulating your blood properly, and you had sufficient nutrients in your body to support the mitochondria, then the Aerobic Metabolism process would most likely be the method of choice for your body to provide energy to your muscles. The mitochondria, of course, are the energy-producing factories of your cells. Let's say, however, that you're running instead of walking. Normally, when our bodies are telling us that they are not comfortable with something we're doing, we stop doing whatever it is we're doing. But, if for some reason, we were tired, but needed or wanted to keep running, but we're gasping for air and the Aerobic Metabolism method just isn't working because we aren't getting enough oxygen fast enough, our bodies will switch over to *Anaerobic Metabolism.* Due to the oxygen debt your body gets from having to use large amounts of oxygen to burn the carbs, fat, and protein for energy, lactic acid begins to accumulate in your muscles. This causes that burning sensation in your muscles and causes you to slow down. However, as you push yourself, and your muscles still need to perform, they began burning more lactic acid and have less of a need for oxygen. This is what is happening to you when you have a *second wind,* that renewed strength and surprising energy you feel when you're exercising or working out. This, of course, also causes more lactic acid accumulation and therefore more burn to your muscles. About 80% of the energy that supplies your muscles is lost as heat. Higher body temperatures, of course, will slow you down and make you tire faster. That's why a lot of people drink sports drinks when exercising or working out - they supply your body with cooling water and energy-producing salts. Although bringing more oxygen into your body and enhancing your circulation gives an additional boost, it's the mitochondria support that makes the big difference in anaerobic metabolism. The third method is the *Phosphagen System.* This system is normally very limited in capability. It's what the body uses when you need sudden bursts of energy. When it is relying on this system, it is burning the *ATP* in your cells. The ATP is made from *Creatine Phosphate,* which is also found in your cells. Very limited amounts of ATP and Creatine Phosphate are stored in your cells, so the energy created is not sustainable for any practical duration. But, your body does have another method for squeezing out more energy. Also called the *fight or flight* hormone, *adrenaline,* or as it is more commonly referred to now, *epinephrine,* is secreted from your adrenal glands under high-stress conditions. It boosts your heart rate, increasing your circulation and breathing rate, which allows more oxygen uptake for more respiration so that a lot of energy is available when needed. Your pupils dilate, improving your vision. Most of your blood supply gets directed to your skeletal muscles and it actually gets restricted from the gut and skin by constriction in these areas. This, of course, slows your digestion. Who needs digestion at a time like this? It speeds up the conversion of glycogen to glucose in the liver. Glucose is the substrate for respiration, which is, of course, energy production. You've heard the stories about a man or woman who actually lifted a car off of their child when the child was pinned under it, right?" Doctor Donovan took another sip of his water. "Yes, along with other amazing tales of super human strength in emergency situations. I've never actually *met* anyone who has done any of those things, though." Cord said. "Well, those things are very real. The region of the brain responsible for maintaining the balance between the stress and relaxation of your body, the *Hypothalamus,* gets stimulated by a stressful situation. When your body is alerted to a situation that could require you to react in such a way that could be above and beyond your normal level of activity, the Hypothalamus sends a signal to your adrenal glands, activating what we call a *Sympathetic System.* This puts your body in an excited state, and your adrenal glands release epinephrine and norepineph-rine, hormones that create this state of readiness that helps us human beings confront and deal with stressful situations. All of these things working together makes us more agile, they allow us to take in more information about our surroundings and use more energy as we need it. The effect epinephrine has on muscles allows them to contract more than usual, giving us, sometimes, amazing boosts in strength. One way to put it, is that we actually have *Superhuman Strength* that is locked away until we are confronted with danger or an extremely stressful or volatile situation." Mark took another drink from his bottle of water. "Well, wouldn't that be just too much on the human body?" Cord asked. "Yes. The duration and magnitude of this strength gained in those situations of the real stories we were talking about, of course, will vary from person to person, and from situation to situation. Scientists have always been looking at our superhuman potential and asked *Why can't we have this all the time?* Our bodies are just not designed to be able to heal themselves, recover, and prevent injury from the constant exertion of superhuman strength. They were designed to deal with, well . . . *regular* human strength. As you and Alan know from working out, developing muscle strength takes time and training. Sudden bursts of muscle use above and beyond the norm can result in injuries such as muscle tearing and even joints being pulled from their sockets. And the harm to the body from remaining in excited states for too long of a duration is tremendous and can cause lasting negative effects, beyond the immediate injuries you may have sustained. Your body goes into a state of exhaustion and begins to wear down. Even your immune system is affected by your body's defenses spending too much time on the stressful situation, making it susceptible to infections and other illnesses. Not to mention an increased chance of just killing over with a heart attack. So, under normal circumstances, it is always better for your body to be in *Homeostasis.*

This is the calming balance created by your hypothalamus. But, of course, *this* study has completely removed you guys from those normal circumstances, right? Progress has already been made over the years in tapping some of that superhuman strength we all have inside of us. We not only have picked up that ball and ran with it, but we've also made a touchdown on keeping your body from tearing itself apart by using that extra strength. The enhancer formula increases your oxygen uptake and speeds up your circulation, which makes your respiration more efficient, it keeps your cells supplied with ATP and creatine phosphate, it reins a tight control on your hypothalamus and adrenal glands and the functions they provide, it keeps the excess lactic acid inert and keeps your body's core temperature lower during energy-demanding tasks. There's even more to it than this, but these are just the things that I am aware of and somewhat understand. There are other things going on and in play that are classified. I don't even know all of it." Mark finished his long lesson, and then gulped down what was left in his water bottle. "How is it possible for your circulation to be faster without your heart rate increasing? How could your cells be supplied with ATP and creatine phosphate at a rate fast enough to accommodate the tremendous energy needed for such remarkable feats of strength? How can . . ." Cord began bombarding Doctor Donovan with questions. "Whoa, hold up there. The *how* is waaaaaay out of my league. And like I said, those things I mentioned are not the only things going on. It's just the ones that I'm familiar with in my part of the study. I know you want even more answers . . . but you can't tell *anyone* that I've told you *anything* in your quest to find them. " Mark said. Cord thanked Doctor Donovan for taking the time to give him such guarded information. Although he wanted more, he left the facility that evening with a good and intriguing feeling of being well informed.

9

Friday, September 25th – 8:00am

The two men met in Andrea's office at 8:00 am. Cord had been on the bubble about the study but ultimately decided to make the study his new temporary employment. The information Doctor Donovan had given him seemed to be sound, and the attraction of maintaining his newly attained, more defined, and sculpted look, coupled with the unbelievable new strength and power of his body had won him over. He wondered if all of the wonderful things happening were somewhat clouding his judgment because he still had a tiny feeling of doubt that would raise its ugly head in his thoughts from time to time. He quickly took a mental hammer and beat it down whenever it came up. He reminded himself of what he and Alan had discussed. *If things begin to seem like they're not quite right, we'll quit. It's that simple.*

"Great! I'm sure you guys are making the right decision!" Andrea said happily. She began tapping the keys on her computer. "Okay, I've given you both clearance for sections 3, 4, and 5. Report to Doctor Strausburg's office in Section 3 on Monday at 8:00 am. You will be working with him for the Stage II enhancer trials." she said. "Will we still be seeing you?" Cord asked. "Well, no. I mean, you may see me from time to time, around the facility. Of course, you're welcome to come see me anytime." she said. "What about Tracie?" Alan asked. "And Doctor Donovan?" Cord added. "Well, the same goes for them. Stage II takes things to a new level. I'm not exactly sure how that part of the program works, but you will be leaving this part behind. I'm sure you can stop in and see them whenever you'd like." she said, smiling. "Well, thanks for everything, Andrea." Alan said, extending his hand. She got up and hugged them both affectionately. "Thank you guys for what you've done for us. Take the rest of the day off. Good luck." she said.

10

Monday, September 28th - 8:00am

Alan knocked on the door to Doctor Strausburg's office, and when he didn't a response, opened the door and stepped through. Cord followed him. Unlike the other offices they had been in so far that were clean and neat, this office looked as if it had been hit by a tornado. There were books, notebooks, and various stacks of paper scattered around, filling whatever space had been available to receive them, including two chairs that were against the wall in front of the doctor's desk. They looked at each other, exchanging amused looks. Within moments, a man stepped into the office, hurrying behind his desk and seating himself. "Please move the papers from the chairs and place them on the floor underneath the chairs and sit down." he said unceremoniously. His accent was thick and sounded to be Russian. His pronunciation of words containing *th* came out sounding like *z*. They both did as he instructed. "I am Doctor Strausburg, as I am sure you are well aware. I will be working with you from this point forward." he said, this time his letter *w* sounding like the letter *v*. He was a short, pudgy man with grey, disheveled hair and a gray and black unkempt beard. He appeared to be in his mid 60's. He wore thick, black-rimmed glasses that were being held together in various places by transparent tape. Unlike the professional appearance of everyone else they had met, the clothing underneath the doctor's white lab coat looked as if he had been sleeping in it. "I do not know exactly what they've had you doing up to this point, but I assure you, we will be working very hard and sloth will not be tolerated for this portion of the study." Doctor Strausburg said as the door to his office opened up. A tall, man wearing a fine, pin-striped Italian suit stepped through the door. He was well-groomed and had an heir of entitlement about him. He had short, straight cut, brown hair, and a pleasant face. "Johannes, you aren't badgering our participants again, are you?" he said. "Uh, no sir. I was just explaining to these gentlemen that this part of the program will be much more involved, and there will not be any room for, as you say, *goofing off.*" said Doctor Johannes Strausburg. "I've read all the reports on these men, and they have really been excelling in the program. I don't think you have any slackers, here. I'm Roberson, by the way, Daniel Roberson, administrator of this program." he said, offering his hands to both of the men. "I'd like to congratulate both of you for your dedication and for remaining with us this far into the program." he added, as he scooted some of Dr. Strausburg's mess over and sat on a corner of his desk. They shook hands in turns. "Very good, sir." said Doctor

Strausburg. It looked as if it was killing him to be polite in the presence of the two men. "What Doctor Strausburg means to tell you, is that with this part of the program, we will have you men performing more practical applications with your new abilities. There will be some hands-on training and scenarios that would relate to real-world situations, other than just your performance levels as determined by your results on our fancy fitness equipment. Of course, the enhancers you will receive in this stage will also be, let's say, upgraded." said Roberson. "What more could our bodies possibly withstand? What else could there possibly be to give us?" Cord asked. "This research is strictly classified! You do not need to know anything beyond what we instruct you to do!" Doctor Strausburg blurted out. Roberson held up his hand and gave Doctor Strausburg an irritated look. Doctor Strausburg closed his mouth and crossed his arms like a scolded child. "Doctor Strausburg is actually correct. We cannot divulge any information pertaining to the contents of the formula. But, Johannes," Roberson said, looking at Doctor Strausburg. "these gentlemen have the right to know what is going on and what to expect." he said, looking back at the two men. "The next stage of the enhancer is formulated for further performance gain, but it also contains some technology that not only assists that performance gain but further addresses the needs of your body. Needs such as mental anxiety and stress, muscle burning and soreness, inflammation, proactive antibiotics, and it virtually stays on top of any problems you may have with potential muscle tearing or joint displacement." Roberson said. "How can *anything* do that?" Cord asked. Doctor Strausburg was turning red and looked as if he were going to explode from Cord's question. "Well, see, that's the thing. We're back into that top secret stuff again. Can't you see how uncomfortable we're making Doctor Strausburg?" Roberson said, smiling and looking over at the doctor. Cord and Alan looked at the doctor, and he was simply glaring at them, his face bright red. "That's Cord for ya. He can't ever leave well enough alone." Alan said, half-jokingly. "Maybe someday for whatever reason, you will have clearance to know the secrets of the enhancer. Maybe not. There's usually a time and place for everything. But as far as the enhancer is concerned, today is not the time, nor is this the place." Roberson said, this time, his smile fading away. Everyone remained quiet for a few moments. Roberson broke the silence. He jumped up from the corner of the doctor's desk, clapped his hands together, smiling once again, and said "Okay, then. I'll let you all get back to work. It was good to meet you two and I hope to see you again soon. Good luck with this leg of the program." he said. Roberson clapped Alan, who was sitting in the chair closest to the door, twice on the shoulder as he let himself out of the office.

Doctor Strausburg dismissed the men right after Roberson had left the room. There was an on-staff attendant waiting outside the door who led them to their living quarters, which were located in section 4. They entered a large door that led into another hallway. Down the hallway, there were several doors with room numbers labeled on each one, not unlike the layout of a hotel hallway. "Alan, your room number is 16, Cord, yours is 27. Your keycards will let you in. Doctor Strausburg wants Alan to report to Doctor Williams' office in the morning at 9 o'clock. Cord at 10." said the attendant. "Why does he get an extra hour of sleep?" Alan said, interrupting the attendant. The attendant continued, ignoring Alan's comment. "His office is located in section 3. Doctor Williams will give you further instructions. You can go ahead and get settled into your rooms. There should be everything you need in there, but if you find something lacking, there's an in-house phone that will connect you with housekeeping." The attendant finished. Alan turned to tell the attendant *thank you,* but the man was already halfway down the hall. "Nice guy." he said. "Well, let's go check out our digs." he added. Cord headed down the hallway toward his room. Alan beeped into room #16 with his keycard. The main light came on automatically as he walked through the doorway into the room. "Sweet." He mumbled. He was quite impressed with the size of the living room. It was much larger than the one he had at home. It appeared clean and smelled good. Although it had somewhat of a clinical feel to it, it also looked rather homey. The furniture and decorations were very tasteful. There was a 42" flat screen TV on the wall, facing the couch. Even though the TV was apparently off, it still displayed the time in large, bold numbers. The kitchen area was clean, bright, and fully stocked with appliances, utensils, and food. There were two bedrooms, both having king sized beds, with full baths. There was a small closet and a 22" flat screen TV on the wall in each room. Each of the smaller TVs displayed the time, just as the larger one had. The rooms were sparsely decorated with a few abstract pieces of artwork that blended with the colors of the comforters on the beds. There were no dressers taking space in the bedrooms, but there were some drawers built into the walls in each closet. Alan lay down on the bed, not even bothering to pull the comforter, and stretched out, yawning. *We haven't even done anything, and I'm tired as heck.* He thought. He closed his eyes.

11

Tuesday, September 29th - 8:03 am

Alan must have been dreaming of a situation with an alarm. He finally opened his eyes and sat up in the bed. There was a loud, repetitive, ringing sound blasting throughout the room. His mouth was dry as a bone, and his already painfully throbbing head was being beat to death by the ringing. He rubbed his eyes and then focused them on the source of the noise. It was the TV on the wall, in front of the bed. It was on and ringing. The time was displayed at the top of the screen with a message below it:

8:03 AM
Doctor William's office
9:00 AM in Section 3

Crap. I don't even remember going to sleep. He thought. He groggily slid off of the bed and switched off the TV. The pain was not just his head: his whole body felt like a train wreck. His back especially hurt like when you've slept on the ground or the hard floor. *Or a strange bed I'm not used to.* he thought. The ringing was still permeating the rooms of his living quarters. He moved slowly at first, like a man with a hangover. He found that both TVs in the bedrooms and the TV in the living room had the alarm and message as well. He switched those off and got some relief from his pounding head. The TVs switched themselves back on, displaying the same information, only this time without the loud, irritating alarm. He made his way to the bathroom. After nature called, he took a hot shower. He found that the hot water really helped alleviate some of the aches throughout his body. *I could really use a massage.* he thought, massaging his own back as far as he could reach. The pain was fading, but of course, his back hurt the most, right where he could not reach it. After showering and brushing his teeth, he went to the closet to get dressed. The only clothes he could find in it, were underwear, bath robes, and some silly-looking, one-piece jumpsuits. He quickly came to the conclusion that the jumpsuit was what he was supposed to wear. *Cord's gonna love this. Looks like some outfit from one of those Sci-Fi TV shows.* he thought. After donning the jumpsuit, he found several pairs of shoes that resembled a popular brand of comfortable slip-on shoes, only these had no identifying marks or brand name. He was impressed that the sizes for his provided habiliments were dead-on. He put on a pair and headed to the kitchen. He noticed that it was 8:48 am. He still had time to grab him a bite. He opened the refrigerator and to his delight, amongst the variety of foods, there was also an assortment of high-protein, pre-mixed nutritional shakes. Although he didn't feel the least bit hungry, he grabbed one, popped it open and sucked it all down without even a pause. He wanted to keep his metabolism going. He then headed to Doctor Williams' office.

Doctor Williams was an older man who appeared to be in his early 60s. He had gray hair and a thick gray mustache. Alan presumed he was actually more of a medical doctor than a scientist, as he had a stethoscope around his neck. "Boy, am I glad to see you, doc. I've felt like I've had a hangover all morning. My body has been hurting everywhere." Alan said. "Step on back to the examination room with me and let's have a look." he said, leading Alan through one of the doors behind his desk. "Hop up onto the table and unzip your jumpsuit down to your waist." said Doctor Williams. Alan did so. The doctor did the same things to him as his family doctor would have done. He listened to his heart. He looked in his eyes, ears, nose, and throat. He pushed on his stomach. He tested his reflexes. He asked him to take deep breaths as he listened to his lungs, with the cold stethoscope on his back. He took a blood sample. "Do you know what's wrong?" Alan asked. "Yep. You can zip your jumpsuit back up." he said. Doctor Williams seemed to be all business. He was a nice enough guy but seemed to have little desire to verbalize anything more than he had to. He began writing notes on his clipboard. "What is it?" Alan asked, mildly concerned. "Nothing to worry about. It's just some of the side effects of the enhancer. You will probably feel fine by the end of the day." said the doctor. "*Probably?* Will I be getting another injection today?" Alan asked. "No guarantees, of course you should know that. You won't need another injection for a while. However, I will be monitoring your blood periodically." Doctor Williams said. "Will I have these side effects again?" Alan asked. "I can't say. People react differently to the enhancer. Take this for your pain." said the doctor, handing Alan a pill and a cup of water. Alan took the pill. *Cord, good luck getting any information out of this guy.* Alan thought. When they walked back out to the office area, Doctor Williams said to report to Training Room A, located in Section 5.Cord stepped out into the hallway of section 4 and headed to Section 3. The extra hour of sleep was not much comfort, but he was glad to have had it, considering his rough morning. He too, had awoke with pains through-out his whole body. As he stepped through the large doors into Section 3, his eye caught a glimpse of a familiar sight, further down the hallway. He sprinted toward the man in the green coveralls, pushing the rolling mop bucket. "Hey, Joe, wait up!" Cord said just loud enough for the man to hear. The man stopped and turned around as Cord approached. "Joe . . ." Cord began. The man was not Joe. A young white man, with black, greasy-looking disheveled hair pulled one of the ear pieces from his ear. Cord could faintly hear the music coming from the unplugged ear piece. It hissed with a fast beat something about killing the financially challenged. "What's up, man?" the young man asked. Cord, slightly embarrassed and surprised, said "Uhh . . . sorry . . . I thought you were someone else." The young man popped the earpiece back into his ear as he said "No problem, man." He turned away and continued pushing the mop bucket down the hallway. Cord turned, disappointed, and headed to Doctor Williams' office.

Much like Alan's visit, Doctor Williams was very brief and

assured Cord that his aches and pains were normal side effects and should subside by the end of the day. He also gave Cord a pain reliever. He instructed Cord to report to Training Room E in Section 5.

It was past 5:00 pm when Alan had finished his first day of practical training. He headed back to the living quarters. He was very tired and still a bit sore. He started to scan his key-card, when he glanced up the hallway and thought about his buddy. *Let me see how Cord's day went.* He walked on up the hallway and stopped at room #27 and knocked. There was no response. He waited a minute, grinned, then pounded heavily on the door. No one answered. *Oh, well.* He went back to his door and went in. He wanted nothing more than to have a hot shower and lie down. He actually did not feel hungry, but the thought of food crossed his mind out of habit. *A nice, hot shower first.*

Cord arrived at Alan's living quarters not long after Alan had stepped into the shower. He knocked on the door labeled #16. After waiting a moment with no response, he tried again. Having no response on the second try, he headed to his room. He was so tired and sore, that he went straight to bed.

12

Wednesday, September 30th - 9:00 am

Both men awoke feeling refreshed and renewed when their TV / Alarms went off this morning. Alan's TV screen directed him to Training Room A, Section 5 once again, and Cord's directed him to Training Room E, Section 5, also the same one as he had went to previously. Their time of arrival was the same, this time: 10:00 am. "Hey, Alan." said Cord. He saw Alan walking down the living quarter's hallway, approaching the door to the Section 3 hallway. Alan turned and stopped, waiting on Cord to catch up. "Whazzup? How's it going?" Alan asked. "I feel a lot better today than I did yesterday." Cord said. "You, too?" Alan asked as they began walking together, heading toward Section 5. "Heck, yeah." Cord said. "Especially my friggin' back." Alan said. "Yeah, mine, too. Not to mention my pounding skull." Cord said. It was only a matter of minutes and they were at the entrance to Training Room A. "Well, this is the room they have me in." Alan said. "What are you doing?" Cord asked. "Learning martial arts." said Alan, shrugging his shoulders as if to add *and I don't know why.* "Me, too, but I'm in Training Room E. I wonder why they didn't just put us together." Cord said. "Don't know. Well, I guess I better get in here." Alan said. "Ok. I'm going to see if I can find out why we we're not able to train together." said Cord. "There you go, make us look like poor schmucks that can't be without each other to hold each other's scared little hands." Alan said, pretending to be annoyed. "Alright, alright, never mind. Maybe we can get together after our training." Cord said. "Great, then we will really look emotionally needy." Alan said, rolling his eyes up, frowning, and shaking his head. "Ok, I'll see you in about a year, around the end of the study." Cord said, sarcastically. Alan began horse-laughing. "See ya." he said through his laughter. "Later." Cord said, smiling. Alan went through the door to Training Room A, and Cord walked on down the hallway, toward his own Training Room.

That evening, after his training, Cord showered and then looked through the fridge and cabinets for something to eat. He realized that he was looking for food out of habit, much like a person who eats when they are stressed or depressed. Again, he was not the least bit hungry, but fixed himself a snack, and pondered about his lack of hunger. He then lay down on the bed to watch TV. The TV did not have standard programming available. There was only a selection of on demand titles available. No commercials or local broadcast. The movie selection, however, was huge. He picked out a Sci-Fi that sounded good and began to watch it. The movie was good, but he just could not focus on it. He switched the TV off, pulled the covers up, and closed his eyes. He wasn't sleepy at all, but he kept his eyes closed. After what seemed like an eternity, he opened his eyes. It was going to be one of those nights. He missed his family. He sat up and climbed out of bed. He slipped on one of his jumpsuits, his slip-on shoes, and grabbed his keycard.

Not even sure where he was going, he found himself at the Fitness Center in section 2. The overhead lights were off, but the colorful LEDs from the equipment and overhead track provided just enough light where he could see and find his way around, so he didn't even bother turning the overhead lights on. He made his way up to the overhead track, beeped the keycard sensor at the beginning of the lane of the track he was going to use, and then began jogging, following the slightly luminescent trail of LEDs that appeared in the floor. He began slowly, as his eyes continued to adjust to the darkness. The only sounds he could hear was the steady hum of electrical equipment in the fitness center, his light footfalls, and his own breathing. He looked behind him to see the footprint trail he was leaving. Each print had different shades of color in relation to the amount of pressure applied to that area of the track by his foot. The footprints were the brightest, closest to his current position. Trailing back a good fifty feet, they gradually faded and disappeared. The faster he would jog, the longer the trail would be. When he would slow down to a brisk walk, the trail would only be a few feet behind him. Andrea was right, the colorful lights up here was beautiful and awesome in the dark. It was so relaxing, the cool air flowing around him as he sped around the track engulfed in partial darkness. He stopped and removed his shoes and began jogging barefoot, so as to see the impressions left by his bare feet. He lost track of time, but he was very glad to have come here. This large room with all of the swirls of color in the dark had somehow lifted his spirits. He still missed his family, but he knew they were okay. He stopped and placed his shoes back on, then headed down to the gym floor below.

Although much less than an average person may have, he had still worked up a little sweat, so he walked into the locker room. He swiped his keycard on dressing room #7, and it beeped. He opened the door and went in, closing the door behind him. He gratefully urinated and then washed his hands. He glanced at himself in the mirror. Just as he began to turn away and look for a towel to dry his hands, he stopped and began looking at himself. He placed a hand on each side of the sink and leaned forward toward the mirror. He noticed that his eyes were a little puffy and barely starting to show dark circles around them. The blood vessels in his head were standing out, as they always had after exercise. His bald head was covered with beads of sweat. He looked older than he did just a couple of months ago. *You can't expect your body to perform like it has been without repercussions.* The little voice in his head said. *I don't really sleep all that well, anyway. I've been working my butt off. I'm under the stress of a new environment. Plus, I've been pumped full of dope.* He thought in an effort to quiet his little voice of reason. *Whatever you say.* it said. He unzipped his jumpsuit, and let it down, exposing his upper body. He finally was looking like one of the ripped guys from a fitness magazine. He ran his hands over his sculpted pecs and abs, feeling no soft spots. He had a strange mixture of pride but was also somewhat ashamed at his own vanity. He pulled the top of the jumpsuit back up and zipped it. He turned on the water once more, and splashed water onto his face and head, vigorously rinsing himself. He shook some of the excess water from his hands, and then opened the cabinet next to the sink and found a stack of towels. He pulled the one from the top of the stack and something fell to the floor with a small *clack*. He finished drying his hands and then dried his face and head. He tossed the towel into a hamper in the corner, and closed the cabinet. He stooped down and retrieved the fallen item that had evidently been carefully placed in his towel. He turned it over and over in his hands, thoughtfully. It was a keycard.

Cord stuck the keycard in one of his jumpsuit pockets and then headed back toward the living quarters. When he let himself into his room, he noticed the time on the living room TV. *1:23 am.* Two more days and he could see his family. They could come Friday evening and stay the whole weekend. As much as everyone needed a break and time alone from time-to-time, he looked forward to seeing his family. He was thinking about them when sleep finally found him and carried him off.

13

Thursday, October 1st -
10:00 am

Cord walked through the door to Training Room E, just as he had every morning this week. This time, Alan was in the room, dressed in a white keikogi, talking to the instructor. Alan turned and saw Cord, smiling. "Okay, whose butt did you kiss and how much did you cry so we'd be in the same class?" Alan asked. "I didn't say anything, I swear." Cord said, surprised. "Having you guys separated for the first few sessions was intentional. Just a little preliminary training and assessment." said the martial arts instructor. Ken Harrison was tall and skinny. He had red hair and a red mustache. He appeared to be roughly the same age as the two men. He was Cord's instructor for the first three days. He had charisma. "Will you be our instructor?" Cord asked. "Yep." he said. "Good." Cord said.

The class went smoothly and both men learned a great deal. Half of the day was spent in discussion of various martial art techniques. The other half was spent with Alan and Cord getting tossed to the floor by Ken and by each other, by one martial art method or another. Ken had informed the men that with the enhancer in their systems, they could take the pain, heal faster, and easily, *literally,* kill him. The point of their sessions was to learn the proper techniques of the art and *how* to fall and how to *recover* from their falls. "If we're supposedly so much stronger than anyone, why bother to learn the proper way to fight?" Alan asked. Ken extended his hand to help Alan up from where he had just launched him over his shoulder. "Well, I have a limited knowledge of the enhancer, but I can tell you the reasoning behind your various training. First of all, you guys are not stronger than *anyone.* Don't think for a minute that we are the only one's working on this technology . . ." Ken began. "Let me guess, this study somehow ties into military applications." Cord interrupted. "That's classified, but could you possibly see how it wouldn't be?" Ken said, smiling. "Even if you *were* the strongest men in the world, we still want you to know how to make the most of your abilities and get maximum performance from them. For example, if your new given abilities allowed you to prevail in a confrontation with four men of your size and stature without any training, just think how many you might be able to beat with the proper training. 8? 10? 12? More?" Ken said. "So we are experimental soldiers." Alan said. "In a way, I guess you could say that. You guys aren't actually soldiers and you won't be going on any missions, I promise you, but what we achieve through this study will help us to determine how quickly a civilian *could* become one. *A performance enhanced soldier.*

And, of course, actual American soldiers are in studies similar to this one, only geared toward training them with other specific skills, taking into account the abilities they already have. In fact, this was a great segue to what I was going to tell you. Tomorrow, we will have a special guest here to train with you. He's actually from one of the earlier military studies." Ken said. "Cool. I guess." Cord said. "Well, you two have a good evening and I'll see you tomorrow morning at the same time." said Ken. "Okay, you have a good one, too." Alan said. They headed to the door. "Cord?" Ken said, before he stepped out the door. "Yeah?" Cord said. "According to my file, you just made it through one more year. Happy birthday!" Ken said. "Hey, thanks." Cord said. "Oh, yeah. Happy birthday, Cord. Darn! Now I owe you lunge." Alan said, pronouncing *lunch* in the silly way the two men do sometimes. They left the Training Room and headed back to the living quarters.

Friday, October 2nd - 10:00 am

The two men had met in the hallway of their living quarters and walked to the Training Room together. As they walked in, they saw Ken talking to a man who had to be the strongest man in the world. Ken seemed to be doing all of the talking, and the man just nodded. The man was about 6 feet tall, weighed about 300 pounds, and was completely ripped. He was wearing jogging pants and an a-shirt, which revealed his unbelievable physique. He was absolutely a monster.

"Hi, guys." said Ken. "This is Brent Houser, or as a lot of people call him, and fittingly, as you see why, *House.* House, this is Cord Grayson and Alan Carson." Ken identified each man with the motion of his hand. House nodded at both men, who nodded back. There was a moment of uncomfortable silence, which Ken broke. "Okay, then, let's go ahead and get started." The first half of the day was very much similar to the previous day. Only this time, it was House who was tossing the men to the floor. And now, across the room. The pain, although easier to handle with enhancer in their systems was still very real, but their recovery was much quicker. They stayed loose and limber, and rolled when they could, just as Ken had taught them. Still, even with the padded floors, they were taking a beating. At lunch time, they took a break. Just as always, Ken brought out a healthy variety of choices and laid them out on a small table with a few chairs in the corner of the room. Ken sat down and began fixing himself a plate. House was not interested in eating, and only walked over to the wall and sat down with his back to the wall while the three men gathered at the table. Alan and Cord both ate for the pure pleasure of eating. Neither man actually had any desire for food. "This is good food and I enjoy eating it, but since that morning I woke up feeling so bad, I've had absolutely no desire to eat. It's as if my body has said *You don't need that anymore.*" Alan said. "You know, I feel the same way. I feel like I've been eating more out of habit than anything." Cord said. "Well, I'm sure the enhancer has made your bodies more efficient at processing your intake. And your digestion has slowed down. But always continue to eat to make sure your bodies always have the energy reserves they need." Ken said. "Yeah, that's true. But we're also burning the heck out of some calories and you'd think we'd be hungry all the time." Alan said. Ken didn't volunteer anything further. They finished their meal in silence.

"Well, I think it's about time for you guys to start tossing House around, huh?" Ken said as he began picking up the plates and utensils they had been using and placing them in a shallow portable basin. Cord glanced over at House, who had just stood up and began doing some stretching exercises. He was just out of ear shot. "Toss him? Both of us probably can't even lift him." Cord said, as he and Alan helped Ken put the remaining dirty dishes in the basin. Ken laughed. "He's a big one, alright. But I think you guys may be somewhat surprised at what you can do. House has been in the program for quite some time now. I don't know all the specifics, but he started in the program when the primary focus was just on size and brute strength. They have made leaps and bounds over the years with the formula. Although you guys may *not* be as strong as House, you've got some other advantages that he does not have. Naturally, his enhancer was modified when applicable, and as the technology progressed, he was given the benefits of it. Unfortunately, however, the earlier enhancers were not as refined as they are now. The effects on health and well being were dramatic in some cases. And irreversible. But, that's really not anything we should be discussing. So, let's get to it." Ken said. He raised his voice so House could hear him. "House, you ready for these men?" House stopped stretching, and stood erect. He simply nodded his head twice and walked to the center of the room on the padded mat. "Not very talkative, is he?" Alan whispered to Cord. "Shoot, maybe he can't talk." Cord whispered back. They walked over to where House was standing. Both men were very uncomfortable. "Ok, boys . . . what're you waiting for? Grab him. Throw him to the floor!" Ken shouted. Alan was a more formidable looking opponent than Cord due to his height and build, but at 6'2" and 235 pounds, he was still nervous. Cord, who was

5'5" and 160 pounds, roughly half of House's weight, was beyond nervous and getting into the scared silly zone. House moved quickly for a man of his size. He let out a grunting yell *yahhhhhh!* as he spread his huge arms, lunged forward, and clothes-lined both men at their shoulders, sending them both backward, and slamming down onto the padded floor. Both men were startled but were quickly back on their feet. This time, Alan did not give House the chance to make another move. He rushed forward, but before he could do anything, House had grabbed him and sent him sailing over his head. Alan went to the floor with a loud thud. Cord rushed in. House simply tightened up and rushed forward like football player, his fists and forearms held up in front of him like a shield. He collided with Cord and sent him sprawling back like a bowling pin. Although Alan and Cord both could feel that familiar rush of their performance enhancers at work, it seemed apparent that size still mattered. Older version of the formula or not: House was kicking both of their butts. Alan had recovered from his slam, and leaped at House, grabbing him around his legs from behind. House went down to his knees, but caught himself with his arms to keep from going down all the way. He intentionally fell to his side, rolling and spinning, slinging Alan free from his legs. He was right back up again. Cord came in again and grabbed one of House's arms and tried to duck around and pull it behind him. All this accomplished was Cord getting himself into a headlock. House had a twisted look of rage on his face. Although he was using only one arm to hold Cord, he was locked in tight.

Cord was not yet able to get free, even using *both* of *his* arms. Alan could see Cord pulling on House's massive arm to no avail. His face was turning red. Alan rushed House and rammed into him, sending him and Cord backwards onto the floor with a loud boom on the mat. House, however, held tight around Cord's head and neck, as they both lay there on the floor. House even curled his free arm around Cord and began squeezing. "Can't breathe." Cord managed to force out with a choked voice. "Let go!" Alan yelled, pulling on House's arms. He could not loosen his grip. Ken ran to a storage closet and came out carrying what looked like some sort of gun. Alan began rapidly hammering House in the face and head with his closed fists. With a sudden explosion, he released Cord and shoved him from atop his body, propelling him a few feet into the air. Cord bounced down beside him like a rag doll. Cord pulled himself to a sitting position and immediately began sucking in air, wheezing and holding his throat. House was quickly on his feet, and approaching Alan. Even though his features were already twisted with rage, you could clearly see that now he was really furious. Ken stepped between them and pointed the device at House and pulled the trigger. There was no sound and nothing visible came from the device. House's shoulder's dropped and he looked to be very limp. He still had the twisted look on his face, but the gusto to drive his feelings seemed to be gone. He just stood there, breathing heavily. "Cord, are you okay?" Alan asked, offering his hand to help Cord stand up. Cord stood up and said "I am now. I wasn't really hurting, I just couldn't breathe." Ken was on the in-house walkie-talkie calling in the incident. A few moments later, two technicians came in and escorted House out of the Training Room.

"Guys, I'm really sorry about that. Are you sure you're okay, Cord? We can have your neck looked at in the infirmary." Ken said. "I'm okay, now." Cord said. "What happened to him?" Alan asked. "I don't know. They took him to the infirmary to draw some blood and run some tests." Ken said. "Will anything like that happen to us?" Cord asked, as he picked up the device Ken had used on House from the table and began turning it over in his hands, examining it. Ken immediately reached out to Cord motioning for him to hand him the device. Cord gave it to him. "Well, what happened to House may have had nothing to do with the enhancers. But, even if it did, you guys have the *good* stuff. The *new and improved,* shall we say. " said Ken, as he placed the device back into the storage closet. "Well, it's my understanding that you guys are having family over to spend the weekend with you, right?" Ken asked. "Yeah, that's right." said Alan. "I hope you guys have a relaxing weekend with your families and I look forward to seeing you again Monday morning. Again, I'm sorry about what happened. "Okay, Ken. You have a good weekend, too." Cord said. They walked out of the Training Room into the hallway.

They began walking toward the living quarters. "Well, at least I'm still alive, right?" Cord said. "No, crap." Alan said. "You know that gun he shot House with?" Cord asked. "Yeah?" said Alan. "It said EMP on the side." Cord said. "So?" Alan said. "Well, EMP usually stands for *Electro Magnetic*

Pulse. To tell you the truth, although I know it's a very real technology, I've only heard of it being used in science fiction movies." Cord said. "Well, we know there's a lot of advanced stuff here." Alan said. "Yeah, but what puzzles me is the fact that an electromagnetic pulse would have little effect on the human body. How could that possibly stun someone like it did House?" Cord said. "Maybe it stood for something else." Alan said. "Yeah, maybe. Thanks for looking out for me in there." Cord said. "Ahh, you would've done the same for me." Alan said. "I couldn't have knocked that big behemoth down." Cord said, laughing. "You would've tried, though right?" Alan asked. "Well, yeah." Cord said. They stopped at Alan's door. "Well, tell everyone *hey*." Alan said. "Same here. Maybe we can all get together tomorrow or something." Cord said. "Okay. See ya." Alan said. "See ya." Cord said. He walked down the hallway toward his room as Alan went into his own.

Alan walked into his quarters. His wife, Faye, was standing in the kitchen drinking a glass of water. "Hey, honey." she said, as she met him in the living room. "Hey, Sweetie." he said, as they kissed. "Duh-dee, Duh-dee!" A little voice traveled up from the couch. His little girl, Hayley, only 19 months old, had stopped playing with the stuffed animals on the couch and looked toward her father, expectantly. Alan scooped her up. "Hey, Sweetpea!" he said as he hugged and kissed her. She smiled with delight. "So, how's the weight training going?" Faye asked. "It's going good. They're currently teaching us martial arts." he said. He made no mention of the fighting incident with House. Although it was nothing to take lightly, he figured it had just happened, and nothing like that would happen again. No sense in causing concern with his wife. Hayley touched her father's face and pulled on his nose. He pretended to bite her hand. "Did you have any trouble finding this place?" he asked. "No, but they treated us like criminals when we came in. They searched all of our stuff. Made me empty my pockets, and had me walk through a metal detector. They wouldn't let me keep my cell phone." she said.

As Cord walked into his quarters, his little boy, Little Cord, who had been watching a movie on the big screen TV, turned and faced him. "Dad!" He ran from in front of the TV straight to his father. "Hey, Captain!" said Cord as he hoisted his son up into his arms. "I missed you, Matey." Little Cord said as they hugged and kissed. Cord walked over to the couch and lowered his son down. His wife, Robyn, who had been reading a newspaper, was watching them. He bent down and kissed her. Little Cord went back to watching his dinosaur cartoon. "How'd it go today?" Robyn asked. "Great. We're learning martial arts now." he said. Cord had also decided not to mention the fact that a huge man tried to choke the life out of him. He did not want to worry her on what was most likely a unique incident. "Are you getting stronger?" she asked. "Every day." He answered, making a Front Double Bicep pose mixed with his own clown-face. He picked up the newspaper laying on the couch, and plopped down next to her. "This the Charlotte paper." he said. "Yeah, I forgot to bring the one from home. I'm surprised I got to keep it. They searched our bags. They kept my camera and my cell phone." she said.

"Yeah, they're real tight with security around here." he said.

Saturday, October 3rd - 2:00 pm

There was a knock on Alan's door. He opened it, and found Cord and Little Cord standing in the hallway, outside his door. "Good grief, there's two of you." Alan said, throwing his arms up. "You . . ." he continued, pointing at Little Cord. ". . . can come in. You . . ." He finished, this time, grinning and pointing at Big Cord, ". . . have to stay outside." He smiled and motioned for them both to come in. "Hey, boys." Faye said. "Hey, Faye. Hey, Hayley." Cord said. "Hey." Little Cord said. Faye was on the couch with Hayley. Little Cord immediately went to Hayley and began talking softly to her and holding her hands. "How's it going?" Alan asked. "It's going good. Robyn wanted to know if she cooked, if you guys would want to come over to eat and maybe watch a movie or something." Cord said. Alan looked at his wife. "Whaddaya think, Sweetie?" he asked. "It's fine with me, whatever you want to do." she said. "Nahhh, I don't think so." Alan said, immediately. Cord's facial expression did not change. He just kept looking at Alan, blankly. Alan busted out laughing. "We'll be there. What time?" he asked. "Six o'clock." Cord said.

The Carson family filed into Cord's living quarters at 6 o'clock. Little Cord and Hayley played in the floor in front of the TV, while a cartoon movie played. Faye began helping Robyn with what was left to do in the kitchen. Alan sat down at the kitchen table. Cord brought him a cold beer and sat down. "Where'd you get these?" Alan asked. "Found them in the 'fridge at the refreshment area in the fitness center at Section 2." Cord said. "Were they for anybody?" Alan asked. Cord shrugged his shoulders as he took a drink. "Does it matter?" he asked, smiling. "No." Alan said, smiling and chugging some of his beer down.

After putting away a few more beers and eating some perfectly cooked filet mignons with all the trimmings, the two couples gathered around the widescreen TV. Cord had started a cartoon movie in one of the bedrooms for Little Cord and Hayley. They sat on the bed quietly, both with wide, round eyes, absorbed by the colorful characters bouncing around on the TV screen. He started a scary movie on the one in the living room, although he was pretty sure no one would actually watch it. They all talked and laughed. Alan and Cord mostly talked about some of their crazy stories from work, the two women talked about kids, clothes, and the like. Alan got up and went to the bathroom. On his way back, he stuck his head in the door to the bedroom to check on the kids. Hayley was lying on her stomach with her rear end stuck up in the air, asleep. Little Cord was sitting next to her, with his hand laid gently on her back, still watching TV. "Hayley's out like a light." Alan said, sitting back down on the couch. "What about Little Cord?" Cord asked. "He's still hangin' in there." Alan said, picking up the newspaper from the end table. Cord stood up and took a few empty beer bottles to the trash. "Want another?" he asked Alan. "Nahh, I think I've had my fill." he said. He paused, then continued. "Hey, isn't this your janitor friend?" Alan folded the Charlotte newspaper he had been browsing through, bringing the photo of interest to the top, and handed it to Cord. Cord's jaw dropped. It was indeed, a picture of Joe, the janitor.

Cord sat on the arm of the couch and quickly read the article next to the picture aloud:

Still missing since late September, Joe Harrison was a faithful member of the "Senior Better Days" club, a local group of senior citizens who gather together twice a month for breakfast, conversation, and bingo. Joe is retired and has no local family. The friends from the club came forward after he missed two consecutive meetings. They looked for him at his place of residence, and found no one home. The superintendent of the apartment building said he has not seen Joe, and it looks as though he has not been in his apartment for some time. If you have seen Joe or have any information on his whereabouts, please contact the police, as they have been notified.

Cord looked at Alan in astonishment. "Don't go gettin' all bent out of shape." Alan said, all too familiar with the look in Cord's eyes. "Bent out of shape? I'm not bent out of shape. I'm friggin' scared." Cord exclaimed. "What's wrong?"

Robyn asked. The women had been chatting amongst themselves, pretty much ignoring the men, until Cord had spoken rather loudly. "We don't need to be here anymore, that's what's wrong. Let's get our stuff and get the heck out of here." Cord said, his voice uneven. He slid off of the arm of the couch, and began to walk toward the bedroom. "Wait, Cord . . . "Alan said, almost in a whisper. Cord turned and said "Alan, I know you don't believe it, and I'm sorry I got you into this mess, but . . ." he began. Alan interrupted him. "Cord – I do believe it. I thought you were over-reacting at first, but *now* I believe. That guy disappearing is just way too much." he said. "So, you're coming, too?" Cord asked. "Yes, but just settle down and stay calm. If you *are* right, do you think they're just gonna let us all walk out of here? Let's hang tight, act as if there's absolutely nothing wrong, and let our families get safely out of here tomorrow. Then, we'll worry about what to do next." Alan said. Cord was impressed. In all his excitement and haste, his mind had currently only been focused on the moment. He knew Alan was right, and waiting was the smart thing to do. Cord had a thoughtful look on his face, and before he could voice his agreement with Alan, Faye spoke. "Okay, you two, what's going on?" she asked. Both men looked at her, and then Cord turned his attention to his wife, who was staring at him impatiently. After several moments of quiet, Robyn said firmly "Cord?" It was more of a statement than it was a question.

They had all settled down on the couch and in chairs, and Cord began telling the account of his suspicions from his first run-in with Joe. Alan chimed in to tell of the discussions between himself and Cord concerning those suspicions. Even Cord admitted, looking back, before this newspaper article, he had begun to wonder why he had been so paranoid. But now, they were both convinced that there was something going on. "Why didn't you tell me?" Robyn asked. "I didn't want you to worry." Cord said. He hesitated and then continued. "And although it was right in front of my face, and I was bringing it to Alan's attention, deep down, I was also trying to convince myself that there was nothing wrong. I was very happy with the results I had when I first started working out with Alan, but when we started this program, for the first time in my life, I felt like I was one of those people that everyone looks at and envies. I didn't want this to end." He finished. "And me?" Faye asked, looking at Alan. "I didn't really think there was anything to worry about. As I said earlier, I figured Cord was over-reacting to the ramblings of an old codger. He has been known to over-react from time to time. The truth is, though, I would have blocked it out, anyway. This isn't something that I would want to give up, either." said Alan.

They had all agreed to act as if nothing was bothering any of them tomorrow, as Alan had suggested. The women and children would get safely out of the facility, and then the men would speak to someone about getting out of the program. If they were not allowed to leave by the next weekend, the women would call the police. It wasn't much of a plan, but it was fairly simple and straightforward.

Faye scooped up Hayley, who had not moved a muscle from where she had fallen asleep. Little Cord had finally drifted off, and stirred slightly when Faye had picked up

Hayley. Everyone said their goodnights and then the Carson family left Cord's quarters and headed to Alan's.

Hayley was in the middle of the king-sized bed, and Faye was watching TV when Alan walked into the bedroom. She turned it off and looked at her husband. He was getting undressed. Normally, he could let things roll off of him with little concern. Tonight, she could see the distress in his face. He pulled his jumpsuit off, turned, and walked toward the light switch, preparing to switch it off. "Wait a minute, Honey. Don't turn that off. Come here." she said. He walked over to her with a smile beginning to spread across his face. "No, Honey. Turn around." she said. "It ain't back there." he said. "Stoop down." she said, ignoring him. Alan felt her fingers touch his back and he jerked lightly. He was a little sore where she had touched him. He stood back up and reached back over his shoulders. He could not reach the area where he had felt the discomfort. "What do you see?" he asked. "There's a scar on your back. I've never seen it before. Did you get hurt?" she said, as she got out of bed. "No." he said, thinking about it. Although the scar was less than an inch long, and very thin, the contrast against Alan's tanned skin made it clearly visible. They walked into the bathroom together. He stood in front of the bathroom mirror, facing away from it. He tried looking over his shoulder, but could not get an optimum view. Faye retrieved a hand-held vanity mirror from one of her bags and handed it to him. He held it up in front of him and angled it so that he could see the bathroom mirror behind him. He saw the small line, approximately halfway up his back. What-ever injury he had incurred, he was completely unaware of it. Although clearly visible now, it seemed to be on the verge of disappearing from the healing process. Had Faye not seen the scar this very night, he may have never known about it. His mind flashed back to not even a week ago when his back had been hurting so bad. He remembered that even Cord had complained about his back as well. "Faye, stay here with the baby. I'll be right back." he said, rushing out of the bathroom, carrying the small vanity mirror with him. "Honey, what is it?" she said, not quite loud enough to wake the baby. "I have a suspicion that Cord has the same scar. I'll be right back." he said, again. He slipped his jumpsuit back on and left the living quarters with Faye's mirror in hand.

Cord opened the door in answer to the repeated pounding. Alan stepped through the doorway from out of the hallway. Cord shut the door. "Sure, come on in." he said, groggily with sarcasm. "Sorry, but this may be important, and can't wait." Alan said. "I thought I was the one who got all excited about everything." Cord said, yawning. "Take off your robe and come with me to the bathroom." Alan said. Trying his best not to smile or laugh. "Don't say a thing." added Alan, as he could see the facetious smile forming on Cord's face as he had been preparing to make a joke. Alan didn't even smile. "*Okay.*" said Cord. "Look, I need to see your back. Take off your robe." said Alan. Cord pulled his robe off and started walking toward the secondary bathroom, so as to not disturb his sleeping family. "Did Robyn not hear me knocking?" Alan asked. "She wouldn't have heard if the walls were coming down around us." Cord said. Cord switched on the bathroom light as he entered, with Alan behind him. Alan had already spotted the scar on Cord's back and handed him the small vanity mirror. "Put your back to the big mirror, and hold this one in front of you, so you can see the big one." Alan said. Cord did as Alan instructed. Although Cord's skin tone was much lighter than Alan's, the scar was still visible. "Okay, hold still. This may hurt." Alan said. He lightly placed his finger on Cord's scar and began to increase the pressure. It didn't take much for Cord to feel it. "Ow!" he exclaimed, as he instinctively reached over his shoulder, but was unable to reach the tender spot on his back. "Do you remember at the beginning of the week, when we both had back aches?" Alan asked. "Oh, yeah." Answered Cord. "Well, somehow, they've done *something* to us." Alan said. "You know, come to think of it, that whole evening was kind of strange. I don't even re-member going to sleep that night." Cord said. "Me neither." said Alan.

16 ▌

Sunday, October 4th -
9:00 am

There was a stirring, and then a slight pressure on his chest. Cord opened his eyes to see his little boy's arms propped on his chest, with his chin resting on them. He was staring at his father. Little Cord was smiling and he smiled back. "Morning, Dad!" Little Cord said. "Good morning, son!" Cord said, putting his arms around his boy and hugging him. Robyn began waking up. "Was that Alan here last night?" she asked. "Yes." he said. He explained the discovery to her and she examined his back. The morning seemed surreal, but the cold reality of his situation began to settle in. *Could this really be happening? Surely, this is a dream. I can't possibly be in the middle of some sort of government experiment and cover-up.* He thought. Little Cord immediately began talking about breakfast. Cord had to convince his son that his mother would take him to get something. He wanted to get his family out of here as quickly as possible. They all worked quickly to get Robyn and Little Cord's things together.

Alan had the same thing on his mind that morning. He wanted his family out of this facility. He hurried Faye along and assisted in packing up their things. Hayley, who was almost always cheerful in the mornings, seemed a little fussy. It was as if she could sense her parents' distress.

Cord and his family entered the hallway to find Alan and his family there, waiting. Everyone was solemn and no one said a word. Normally, Little Cord would have been trying to get to the baby. Instead, he was glued to the side of his father's leg. "Okay, we've all got to cheer up. Everything's going to be fine." Alan said. Nothing changed. "Let's go." Cord said. They all shuffled down the hallway. They arrived at the guard station, where the guards checked their bags. "Honey, you've got that fine silverware from the kitchen hidden good, right?" Cord asked aloud, winking at his wife. Robyn simply looked at him, shaking her head. Once the baggage was cleared, the families said their goodbyes. "Oh, I need to get my camera and cellphone." Robyn said to one of the guards. "Yes, and my cell phone." Faye added. The guard looked through the desk he was standing behind. "There's nothing here." he said. "Well, they said that I couldn't take it in, and told me I'd have to leave it here." she said. "I understand that, ma'am, but there's nothing here, now." he said. "Listen you wannabe cop, she left a camera and a phone here and she wants it back!" Cord exclaimed quietly so as his son would not hear, as he stepped forward. For the first time, Cord noticed that the guards were not only wearing guns, but also a device like the one their martial arts instructor had, tucked in their belts. Was it his imagination, or did the guard actually move his hand toward his gun as Cord had stepped forward? "Sir, I'm sorry, but there's no camera or phone here." he said. "Get Dr. Lawson on the phone." Cord whispered. The guard complied. Once the call was connected, he handed the receiver to Cord. Cord explained the situation to Andrea. She apologized and assured Cord that they would replace the camera and the cell phone. "One more thing, Dr. Lawson." Cord said. "Yes?" she asked. "Do you think I could meet with you to go over a few things?" Cord asked. "I told you now that you're in stage 2, you really should talk to Dr. Strausburg." she said. "I'd really rather talk to you. You did tell us we could come to see you any time, remember?" he said. "Yes, of course, if you need to see me, you can." she said. He handed the receiver back to the guard. One of the guards buzzed the door for the women and children to pass through. Cord and Alan said their goodbyes to their families and then walked to the refreshment area of the Fitness Center to round up something to eat. They were both wondering what to do next.

"We could always just beat up the guards and bust out." Alan said. They were sitting at one of the tables in the refreshment area, having breakfast. "Well, no doubt, we could literally pulverize the guards, but they were carrying guns and those EMP guns, too, like the one Ken Harrison used on House. I don't know how, but I have a feeling that those things may work on us, too." said Cord. "I bet the EMP things have something to do with what's happened to our backs." Alan said. "Yeah, I think you're right. But *what* exactly *have* they done to us?" Cord said.

"This is Doctor Strausburg. Why are you calling me on a Sunday?" said the doctor, with his thick accent. "Doctor Strausburg, this is Officer Farris. We had a minor incident here this morning." The guard said. He explained what had happened with the camera and cell phones, and the fact that Cord had requested to talk to Doctor Lawson. "How did you manage to lose a camera and some cell phones in two short days?" Doctor Strausburg asked. "We didn't actually lose the items, sir. We've recently been given strict orders to confiscate any items related to recording and /or communications." said Officer Farris. "But these items were checked in with you before they entered the facility, correct?" said the doctor. "Yes sir, but our orders did not specify any stipulations on the confiscations." said the guard. "You should have known that if you've had their devices, there was no way they could have been used or collected any information. But, I know you were just following orders. What exactly did Mr. Grayson say to Doctor Lawson?" asked Doctor Strausburg. "All I could make out was that he wanted to see her and talk to her. Our orders to restrict their calls do not apply to facility personnel." said the guard. After a moment of silence, Doctor Strausburg said "You did good to contact me, officer." Officer Farris gave his co-worker a big, grin, in reference to his fawning on Dr. Strausburg. "Thank you, sir. I'll call you back if anything else should come up." he said. He hung the phone up.

17

Monday, October 5th - 9:00 am

Alan was sleeping like a rock when the TV alarm began blaring. It displayed the time and alerted him that he was to meet in Doctor Strausburg's office at 10:00 am. He knew something was up, because they were supposed to be going to martial arts this morning. *Surely this meeting was not a result of the few select words Cord had with the security guard. But if not, then what could it be about? How could **they** know that **we** knew what was going on? Or think we do.* Alan thought. He headed to the bathroom for his shower, still puzzling over what was to come.As Cord sat up in bed and stared at the TV screen that had sounded the same information alarm, the same thoughts went through his head as did Alan's. Unlike Alan, he had not slept well at all that night. Not only was his mind puzzled, but it was tired, too. He pushed himself through the motions of showering and getting ready to go to the meeting. After he donned his jumpsuit, he retrieved his keycard and slipped it into his pocket. After a quick breakfast, he left his quarters, where he met Alan in the hallway. They headed to Doctor Strausburg's office.

Doctor Strausburg was sitting behind his desk, waiting for them. He got straight to the point. "It has come to my attention that there was a problem Sunday morning when your families were leaving the facility." he said as he leaned forward. He had the air of a strict principal interrogating students who had been suspected of bringing a weapon to school. "Yeah, there was a problem. The security guards *lost* some of our families' things." Alan said sharply, enunciating the word *lost*. "Policy strictly forbids bringing communication or recording devices into the facility. You should be fully aware of this policy, as should your families. We simply ask that they leave these things behind when they come for visitation." said Doctor Strausburg, with a simple, matter-of-fact attitude. "Well, maybe they won't be coming back for visitation." Cord said. "And maybe we won't be staying, either." Alan said. Cord looked at Alan with surprise. He knew Alan wanted this more than he did. "We have a contract!" exclaimed the doctor. "Contracts are broken all the time." Cord said. "Not these." Doctor Strausburg said cooly. "Are you saying that you won't let us go? You'll try to keep us here against our will?" asked Alan. There was a brief silence. "Of course not. But if you do decide to break your contract and leave, you must be processed out. There are no exceptions to this for safety reasons." said Doctor Strausburg. Some of the wind seemed to be leaving his sails. "Well, when can we start processing?" Cord asked. "Please gentlemen, I feel that you would be making a grave mistake over a simple misunderstanding. We have come so far with you in the program, and we would all lose so much if you left. Let me at least call Mr. Roberson to talk with you before you make any rash decisions." Doctor Strausburg said. His whole attitude had shifted. He no longer had the attitude of the strict principal, but the meekness of the guilty student. Alan and Cord looked at each other. They both nodded. "Okay, fair enough." Alan said. "Alright, then. We will hold off on your training until we get this situation straightened out. When I can get in touch with Roberson and arrange a meeting, I will let you know. Thank you, gentlemen." The doctor said, as he stood up. Cord and Alan stood and left his office.

The two men headed to the fitness center and spent the rest of the morning working out. There was none of the usual joking and laughter. Both men were in very somber moods. After their workout, they went to the refreshment center for lunch. Both men were quiet during their meal as well. After they had eaten their lunch, Alan said "I think I'm gonna just go back to my quarters and watch a movie. This whole thing has got me on edge." Cord nodded. He hardly ever saw Alan rattled. "I think I could use a nap, myself. I didn't sleep very well last night for the same reason." Cord said. The two men left section 2 and went to their quarters in section 4. They stopped at room #16. "Well, if I don't see you later today, I'll see you in the morning." Alan said as he beeped his keycard for his door to open. "Alright, Alan. I'll see you later." Cord said. Alan went into his room. Cord continued down the hallway to room #27. He beeped his door open and went in.

He dropped his keycard on the kitchen counter and slipped off his jumpsuit. He walked to the bathroom, preparing to toss the jumpsuit into the pile of other dirty jumpsuits lying in the floor. He changed his mind and found the hamper. He tossed the jumpsuit in the hamper and began picking up the others. As he did so, he felt something in the pocket of one of them and remembered the keycard that he had found in his dressing room at the facility's fitness center. He put it to the side and placed the remaining jumpsuits in the hamper. He picked up the keycard and carried it with him over to his bed. He lay down and closed his eyes. He was too tired to worry about anything right now. He was soon fast asleep.

18

Tuesday, October 6th -
3:27 am

Alan rolled over in his bed. He was surprised at how his conscious mind was even able to determine how realistic sounding the call of his name was in his dream state. *"Alan."* He could hear his name so clearly in his dream. *"Alan."* The voice in his dream sounded so familiar. "Alan!" It was getting louder. *"Alan, get your butt up!"* Alan sat bolt upright in bed. *This is no dream . . . it's a nightmare.* he thought. He was a little startled but quickly realized that the silhouette of the person that was standing in his bedroom doorway was Cord. "What the heck are you doing here?" Alan asked. *"How* the heck did you *get* in here?" he added. "I forgot to tell you about this keycard I found in the dressing room. It was placed in my towels as if someone had left it for me. It seems to be able to access *anywhere.*" Cord said. "Okay. Well, that explains the *how* part. What about the rest?" Alan asked. "We're gonna try to get out of this place." Cord said. "We don't have to try.

Doctor Strausburg said we could be processed out after we talk to Roberson, remember?" Alan said with sarcasm. "Look, we know they've already done something to our backs without telling us about it. I don't trust them. I think they're just stalling for time. They've probably already got plans for what they're gonna do with us . . . and *to* us." Cord said. Cord's statements were simply confirmations of the gut feelings Alan already had.

They stood at the doorway at the end of the hallway of their living quarters that led to the front entrance. Cord reached for the handle. "Wait." Alan whispered. "How are we going to get past the guards when we get there?" he asked. Cord pursed his lips. "Right. Let's not go this way. There has to be another way in and out of this place. They have to receive supplies from somewhere other than the door we usually come in and out of. Remember, there are a few other doors to the building, and there was a loading dock." Cord replied in a whisper. "Okay, but it seems like a pretty crappy plan." Alan whispered, grinning. "It's all I got." Cord whispered back. They headed back the way they came and crept through the doorway into the main hallway for Section 4.

The hallway was quiet and deserted. They went to the right and headed to the end of it. Cord beeped the door and they entered Section 5. The main hallway for Section 5 was just as still and empty as the one they had just left. They passed several offices and training rooms before they got to the end of the Section 5 hallway. "Okay, this is as far as we've ever been in the facility. We don't have a clue of what's on the other side of this door." Cord whispered, looking at Alan.

Alan nodded. Cord beeped the door. They stepped through into Section 6. Instead of the familiar hallways they were used to seeing as they entered one section or another, this time the doors opened up into what looked like any hospital the two men had ever been to. Clean, white tiled flooring. Medical equipment was setup in various locations. It even smelled like a hospital. They figured it was a medlab of some sort. They cautiously glanced around before proceeding further into the hospital area. Evidently no one was here, because only a few of the smaller fluorescent lights were on, giving just barely enough light to see. It was not deathly quiet in this area as it was down the other hallways, as there were the hums of various pieces of equipment throughout the area. There were eerie shadows cast all around by the equipment. Some of the equipment had faint beeping noises coming from it, with intermittent, blinking lights. They both stepped softly and proceeded across the hospital area in the direction opposite the door they had entered. The hospital area had several rooms off to the sides and various aisles to go down, but nothing seemed like a dedicated hallway to lead you to the other side, there were only wall partitions here and there. Everything was too tall to see over. Cord was leading the way, with Alan only a few steps behind. He was choosing what he thought was the best path down the aisles that would lead them across the large room, through the maze of cubicles and equipment. A few minutes into their walk, he turned to check on Alan, but Alan was gone. He quickly tried retracing his steps but could neither see nor hear Alan. "Alan!" he whispered as loud as he dared. Cord was no longer sure which way he had come and where he was. He picked up his pace and began maneuvering around the partitions and equipment a little faster. "Alan!" he shouted in a whisper. As he turned the next corner, he ran right into a gurney. This scared him, but he did not get hurt. "Cord!" Alan shouted in a whisper, as he walked up behind him. Cord jumped. "Dang it! You scared the heck out of me." Cord said. "Look what I found." Alan said. He laid two file folders on the gurney and opened them. One was labeled Alan Carson and the other Cord Grayson. It was their medical files. Alan pulled out a couple of x-rays from his file and held one of them up toward one of the small fluorescent lights. Although the lighting was poor, there was no mistaking the fact that there was a tiny object next to the spine on the x-ray. "What is it?" Cord asked. Before Alan could answer, the lights came on, startling both men.

"It looks like a prototype of a modified, miniature nano-wired battery." a nearby voice said. Both men jumped. As they began looking around to find the source of the voice, a man walked up to them. They had both thought that the voice had sounded familiar. It was Mark Donovan, the first doctor that had begun administering the enhancers to them at the beginning of the program. "Mark, you scared the heck out of us." Cord said. "What are you guys doing in here? And *how* did you get in here?" Mark asked. Cord and Alan looked at each other. "We're trying to get out." Alan said. "What are *you* doing here at this hour?" Cord asked. "Well, unlike you guys, I am authorized to be in this area . . ." Mark began. "Bullcrap. You're down here helping yourself to more juice." Alan said. Mark opened his mouth to quash Alan's remark, but remembered that he was holding three vials of the enhancer in his hand, in plain sight. He looked down at the vials as he closed his mouth. "We knew you were taking the juice when we first met you. We don't care. Why should we? Right now, we just want to get out of here." Cord said. "Why do you want out so bad that you're trying to sneak out in the middle of the night?" Mark asked. "These for one thing." Alan said as he tapped the x-rays lying on the gurney. "Yeah, why the heck did they put batteries in our friggin' backs?" Cord asked. "And it would have been nice for them to let us know what they were planning on doing." Alan said. "Look, I don't know a whole lot about what goes on in the program beyond the use of the Stage I Enhancers. What I went over with you, Cord, pretty much sums up my knowledge of the part of the program that I'm involved with." Mark said. "Are you sure that's what it is? A battery?" Alan asked. "No, I'm not positive, but I've seen devices similar to that over the years in my work, and that looks pretty darn close. I swear to you, I am completely unfamiliar with any other testing they have done with you since they moved you from my section. I am sorry that they seem to have not been straight up with you." Mark said. "This goes way beyond just not being straight up with someone." said Alan. Between Alan and Cord, they filled Mark in on what had been going on, and their talk with Dr. Strausburg. "I'm not so sure that I want to leave just yet. Now that I know what's next to my spine, I don't know if I want to go running off until I figure out what to do." said Cord. "But, how much longer can we stay here before they really screw us up good?" asked Alan. "And we're worried about our families." Cord added. "Look . . ." Mark said. He hesitated, trying to select his words carefully. ". . . I think that you guys may be over-reacting just a little bit." he continued. Alan and Cord both began protesting at the same time. "Wait, wait, wait. Hold on . . ." Mark interrupted, as he held his hands up defensively. "I know the mystery surgery to the back doesn't seem quite appropriate, but you need to remember, your contracts were wide open. I skimmed through them myself. There was so much material in there, I didn't even dare an attempt to actually *read* it. It did, however, look to me as if they practically owned you two outright and could do whatever they wished to do. That still doesn't make *how* they handled it *right*, by any means. But, I would not think there was any *real* monkey business going on." Mark said. "Well, that's easy for you to say. You're not the one who had a battery jammed in your back." said Alan. Mark looked around solemnly. "Let me see what I can find on one of these terminals." he said, leading them to one of the dark offices in the medlab. The particular medlab office they entered was Dr. Strausburg's. It was obvious that Mark had been helping himself to this terminal before, as he used Dr. Strausburg's login name and password, which was written plainly on a sticky note stuck to the monitor. He logged in and began tapping away at the keys. Screens of information began popping up. Some had photos of Alan, and others of Cord. There were medical files, x-rays, and other documentation. "Aha!" exclaimed Mark, quietly. "What?" Cord asked. "Well, I've never really had the need to do any digging beyond some of the basics, but I've found links that are taking me deeper into the enhancement program." said Mark. Alan and Cord drew themselves closer around Mark and the computer where they could have a better look at the screen. "You two are in the study called *Project Nemesis*." Mark said. "What does that mean?" Alan asked. Mark continued typing and then said "**Nano-technologically Engineered Muscularly Enhanced Surgical Implantation System.**" Cord and Alan looked at each other. "Nanotechnology?" Cord asked. "Yes, that term references *nanobots*. Those tiny, microscopic robots." said Mark. As he would pull up new information that was pertinent to Project Nemesis, he would read the text and then give it to them in layman's terms. "It seems that I was right about the battery. They're using it in this circumstance to keep nanobots charged, although they apparently receive some of their power from your own nervous systems." said Mark. "So, do we have those robots inside of us now?" Alan asked. "I don't know yet." he said, typing and reading quietly. "How does the battery charge nanobots?" Cord asked. "They can be continually charged simply by being in the vicinity of the battery, but of course they are subsidized by the electricity generated by neurons which result from the motion of sodium and potassium ions across the cell membranes. Are you guys familiar with a charging plate?" Mark asked. "Yes, it's just a small, flat pad that you can simply lay your cellphone, mp3 player, or whatever, on top of it and it charges them. No wires at all." Cord said. "The battery uses the same concept." said Mark. He wiggled the mouse and clicked some more keys. "Okay, you don't have the nanobots in you yet, they're scheduled for injection next week." he said. "That's a relief." said Alan. Mark continued tapping on the keys of the keyboard. "Yes, it is a relief. From just what I gather here, it seems the nanobots work with and *within* your body, giving you tremendous strength and abilities on demand, or . . . it is possible that your body totally rejects them as if they were a virus and reacts with a cytokine storm, which can make you very sick and could possibly kill you. It must be treated immediately. They have many different drugs they are currently working on for the ones whose bodies reject the nanobots. They also have the ability to travel within the body to assist the body with the quick regeneration of damaged tissue, along with other remarkable things." Mark said, scanning the text in front of him. Alan and Cord stepped back from the terminal so that Mark could stand up. "You know what? I think I know where they keep those little rascals." he added, as he stepped out of Doctor Strausburg's medlab office. Alan and Cord followed him. He led them to another office in the medlab. Not only did he have to use his keycard, but he also had to enter a numeric code on a keypad to gain access. They followed him in. "This is where they keep these," he said, holding up the vials of enhancer. He walked up to one of the shiny, polished metal cabinets in the room, and placed his hand on it in designation. There was another, similar cabinet next to it. He turned to this cabinet and swung the double doors open. The interior of the cabinet was locked up like Fort Knox and seemed to be built of some sort of thick, polished plexiglass material, which allowed you to see the contents inside. The shelves were full of vials of what appeared to be a silvery, swirling liquid. The very top shelf was empty, with the exception of two oversized, expensive-looking hypodermic syringes. They were each up on their own little pedestals. These syringes appeared to have the same contents as the vials but also had an eerie yellow glow pulsating from within. This internal luminescence gave the silvery, swirling liquid the appearance of a living organism. The three men watched hypnotically. "Those two syringes weren't there the last time I looked into this cabinet." Mark said, quietly. There was no doubt as to who these syringes were intended for.

"Look, guys, I don't want you to end up in any trouble, or put any additional risks to your health. From what you told me, they wouldn't dare do anything else until after Roberson has spoken with the two of you. You can go ahead with your attempt at leaving tonight, and I promise you, I won't say a word to anyone. As you know, I'm not supposed to be here anyway. Or, you can wait, and I'll dig around and see what else I can find to try and help you figure this thing out. I can nose around the labs, and do more digging into the computer system." Mark said. Alan and Cord looked at each other, as they all exited the secured room and went back into the main part of the medlab. "I guess it would make more sense to wait. This thing in our back may be something we want to have removed before they release us." Cord said. "And on the other hand, if we wait, we may be giving up our only opportunity to get out of here." Alan said. Everyone was momentarily silent. Cord broke the silence. "I think our biggest concern is the safety of our families. If we stay, could you get a message to someone for us?" Cord asked. "I could do it first thing in the morning." Mark said. Mark handed Cord a pen from his pocket and pulled an old receipt from his wallet. Cord wrote on the back of the receipt and handed it and the pen back to Mark. "Okay, guys. I'll get in touch with you as soon as I find something." Mark said. Cord and Alan began maneuvering their way back through the maze of equipment, back toward the doors they had entered. Mark disappeared back the way he had come.

19

Tuesday, October 6th -
10:00 am

10:00 AM
Doctor Strausburg's office
11:00 AM in Section 3

The TV / Alarm blared out as it displayed the information on the screen. Both Alan and Cord were directed to Dr. Strausburg's office this morning. Both men dressed and met in the hallway.

Cord pushed the door to Doctor Strausburg's office open and walked in, with Alan right behind him. Daniel Roberson was sitting behind Doctor Strausburg's desk, doing something on the computer. He didn't even look up when the men entered the room. They stood silently for a few moments, then Alan cleared his throat. Roberson typed a few more keys, clicked a few more mouse clicks, then looked up and said "Ahh, yes. If it isn't my two favorite lab rats." All pretense of the pleasant, professional businessman was left behind. "I've heard that you two are unhappy and wish to get out of your cages, is that correct?" Roberson asked. Cord and Alan looked at each other, reading each other's thoughts. *Who the heck does he think he is?* "We're not in cages, but yes, we want out of the program." Cord said. Roberson looked away, slowly nodding and pursing his lips together. "Everything was going so well, until your families had to make a big deal over petty items that they were explicitly told not to bring to the facility in the first place." Roberson said with disgust. Alan and Cord both flushed with anger and began stepping forward toward Roberson. Roberson didn't look the least bit concerned with their approach. "Not a good idea." he said, holding his hand up. Both men stopped. "You see, there are only four ways to get out of this program. The first is if the side effects are so extreme that they render you useless to us. The second is if you actually *die* from the side effects. The third way is if you're good little rats, you cooperate, go through all our little mazes and jump through all our little hoops, and the testing doesn't kill you, you get to continue to work *within* the program in some capacity. The fourth . . . well, the fourth is really the ugliest. It's when test subjects want to be little cry-babies and run home at the first sign of trouble." Roberson said these things with disdain in his eyes. He continued. "And it seems to me, that we just might be approaching the fourth way, gentlemen. Are we approaching the fourth way?" he asked. Before either man could respond, Roberson shouted "THIS IS YOUR NEW LIFE, AND UNLESS YOU WANT SOME VERY UNPLEASANT BUSINESS TO BE HANDLED, I SUGGEST YOU CONTINUE TO BE GOOD LITTLE

RATS AND COOPERATE!" His sudden outburst startled the men. He used his free hand and swiveled the monitor on Doctor Strausburg's desk around, so it was facing the men and then brushed by them and walked out of the office, not saying another word. Alan and Cord simply stared at the monitor. There were two opened windows on the computer screen, positioned side-by-side. They were live video feeds of both men's homes. There was no doubt about the implication of Roberson's message.

20

Tuesday, October 6th - 11:08 am

Their spirits crushed, the men left Doctor Strausburg's office and headed to Mark Donovan's office, which was in section 2. When no one answered the door, Cord looked around and then used his extra keycard. The two quickly slipped into Mark's office and closed the door. As they were nosing around his office, Alan said "Cord, come look at this." Cord walked over to Alan, who was standing behind Mark's desk. Alan was looking down at Mark's desk blotter. Cord followed his gaze and saw the blood droplets across the blotter and various papers which were scattered across the desk. "Oh, no." Cord said in a whisper. They quickly left the office and headed back toward their living quarters.

21

Tuesday, October 6th -
4:00 pm

Jason Kaiser turned the orange 1991 muscle car into the gravel driveway that led up to Cord's home. He immediately noticed the shiny, black sedan parked off of the street in front of the house, and thought that it looked rather odd and out of place. He slowly rolled up the driveway, which wound around behind the house, the only sound being the *blub-blub-blub* of the engine. He parked, got out, went to the back door and knocked. Robyn came to the door. "Hi, I'm Cord's friend and co-worker, Jason Kaiser. I need to talk to you." said Jason. "I remember meeting you before." Robyn said and let him in and they walked to the living room, where Little Cord was playing with some small cars. He looked up. Jason said "Hey, Buddy, remember me?" Little Cord got up and gave Jason a hug. They sat down, and Little Cord sat right next to Jason. "Look, Cord sent me this note which tells me that he and Alan are in some kind of trouble. All the note said was that they were scared for their families' lives and could I please get you all and take you somewhere safe. Some doctor brought it to my house this morning." Jason said. Robyn nodded and quickly filled him in on the downturn of the study and the business of the missing janitor who had given them a warning. She told him about the mysterious scars on both of their backs, and the incident that had happened with the cell phone and camera when the families had left the facility. "Yeah, they had told me a little about the study that they were participating in. I really thought it was too good to be true when they told me that they were temporarily leaving their jobs to spend more time in the study." said Jason. He stood up and went to the living room window and peered out through the blinds. "Did you know there was a car parked out front?" he asked. Robyn stood up and walked to the window and peered out as well. "No, I didn't." she said. "Go ahead and gather you and Little Cord some things together and let's head out." he said. Robyn grabbed some extra clothes for Cord and herself, a few toys for Cord, and their medicines, not knowing how long they would be gone. She put them in a bag, and they all headed out the back door. Robyn got in the back with Little Cord and they buckled their safety belts. As they pulled out of the driveway onto the road, the black sedan's lights came on, and it pulled from the roadside and made no secret that it was going to follow them.

Jason headed to Alan's home. When they arrived, they immediately noticed another black sedan parked in front of the apartment building. The one that had been tailing them, kept its distance. The three of them went to Alan's door and Jason knocked. Faye came to the door. She recognized Jason, but was a little startled seeing the three of them together standing at the door. She immediately knew something was wrong and quickly let them in. Jason explained the note that had brought him to collect the families. He also told her about being followed by the black sedan and the fact that there was another one sitting outside, watching them right now. Faye gathered extra clothes for herself and Hayley, along with some toys, some of the baby's food, and the diaper bag. "Look, let's wait until late night to early morning to make a run for it and try to lose those guys. Maybe it will throw them off and they won't be prepared. Maybe they'll be asleep. Shoot, maybe they won't even stay." said Jason. "That's a lot of *maybes*." said Faye. "Yeah, but it's all we got." he said.

22

Tuesday, October 6th -
6:00 pm

"What are we going to do?" Cord asked Alan. They were in Alan's living quarters, pacing back and forth in the kitchen area. "I don't know, Cord. I'm sorry I didn't listen to you when you first had your suspicions. Maybe we would not be dealing with this right now." Alan said. "Yeah, but I'm the one who got us into this mess to start with. I have a feeling, that regardless of *if* and *when* we decided to bail out of the program, things would have still played out the same. Like that creep said, *you can never leave.* They already had too much invested in us as test subjects to let us go. I don't think there was ever really any option to leave the program." Cord said. "I know our number one concern is for our families. By Roberson showing us that our homes are under surveillance, he was basically threatening that he would harm them if we didn't cooperate. But, you know what? I think that was probably on the agenda anyway. I'd rather take my chances *now,* while I'm alive and kicking, to try and do something, rather than live in the program, wondering if something goes wrong and I die, if they're gonna make our families have mysterious accidents or disappear to tighten up any loose ends." Alan said. "If I had a strong feeling that our families would be safe from our cooperation, whether we died from the program or not, then I'd disagree with you. But I think you're absolutely right. I'd rather take my chances trying to get to my family, rather than staying here, wondering, too. Let's do what we should have done last night . . . wait until early morning and then get the heck out of here." Cord said.

23

Wednesday, October 7th -
3:15 am

The two men had slipped their street clothes back on and went the same way they had went the previous night. They were quiet and cautious, never encountering anyone. Once they were in the medlab, Cord looked at Alan and said "How about not wandering off this time?" Alan grinned. They made their way through the mazes of equipment and office cubicles. They finally came to some unmarked double-doors. Cord waved his extra keycard over the keypad and there was a beep. Instead of swinging, these doors slid into the walls, like the doors on a spaceship in a science fiction movie. The two men walked through the doorway.

The doors slid shut behind them. This area seemed to be a preparatory room of some kind, to outfit you with various gear of your choosing, before you continued into the next section. There were biohazard suits, gloves, protective face shields, shock-sticks, rubber boots, plastic aprons, and other items designed to help keep you safe and clean. There was another set of double-doors on the other side of the room. They proceeded forward and beeped their way in.

As the doors slid open, they were hit with the familiar odors of past visits to zoos and county fairs. There was the pungent smell of animals, mixed with the smell of various feeds, and, of course the smell of animal feces mixed in to top it off. "Dang." Alan said. Both men let their olfactory senses adjust a little bit, then walked through the doors. The lights were dim, and they could see the reflective glow of eyes looking at them from along the walls. "This is section 7, I believe." Cord said. "I call it *Section Stinky.*" Alan said. Section 7 for the most part, was a long hallway with various cages along the walls housing different species of animals. There were doors scattered and spaced out along both sides of the hallway as well. As they walked down the hallway, a few of the animals were disturbed at their presence. They showed it by growling, hissing, snorting, screeching, or frantically shuffling around in their cages. Most of them, however, either ignored them, or slept. They passed dogs, cats, rabbits, small pigs, and small primates. Most of the doors along the hallway were small offices with glass panes, which allowed them to see in. As they passed by them, they would stop and peer in. All of them were basically the same, with a desk, a computer, a couple of file cabinets, a small examination table, a couple of free-standing, tall cabinets, a few chairs, and a large sink. They passed one door labeled *Large Animals.* As they approached another door, Alan stopped and said "Did you hear that?" Cord had stopped walking and stood very still and very quiet.

After a moment, Cord heard it, too. It sounded like a person moaning, as if they were in pain. "It's coming from there." Cord said, pointing at the door they had just approached. The door was identical to the one they had just passed labeled *Large Animals,* only this one had no identifying marks on it. Alan reached out and pulled on the handle, but the door did not open. "Try your keycard." he said. Cord swiped the card, and the door beeped open. Although still barely audible, the moaning was a little louder. They cautiously went through the door. It was an entrance to another hallway. It was dank, dark, and musty, much like they imagined a dungeon might be. Unlike a dungeon, however, the floor was smooth, glossy concrete instead of flagstones. The dim, flickering light came from a faulty ballast in a fluorescent light, instead of a torch. But the small rooms with iron bars and locked gates lining each side of the hallway could not have been much different than a dungeon's. The first few cells were empty, save for some dirty straw on the floor, scattered around a drain in the center of each of them. The first resident they saw from this dungeon was a chimpanzee. It almost looked fake, as it was swollen up like a balloon. It was lying on it's back in the center of the dirty cell. It's eyes were vacant, and it breathed in quick, shallow breaths. "Oh, my." Alan said. Both men were horrified at the display. It was all Cord could do to keep from running in terror, but he knew there could be someone in here that needed their help. He hoped they could help the nimals. "Come on." Alan said. Cord forced his feet to continue forward. The next few cells were empty. The moaning got a little louder. The next occupied cell contained a dog. The two men could not tell what breed, because of the lighting and the disfigurement of the animal. At their approach, the dog forced itself up on to trembling legs. It's head was so disproportionately large, it could not lift it. As it pulled itself toward the gate, possibly expecting to be fed, it dragged its head, which was turned to the side from the excess weight. It still managed to wag its tail a few times to greet it's visitors. Alan covered his mouth to stifle a scream of sorrow. Cord rubbed his eyes where they had began to spill hot tears. Although neither man was a real animal lover, seeing these creatures in these conditions began a hot anger boiling inside of them for whoever was responsible. "I can't believe this." Cord said. They shuffled forward and again, the next few cells were empty. As they approached the next occupied cell, there was a fierce, ear-splitting cry of rage, which scared them so badly they jumped back from the bars. A large, dark, furry figure rushed the gate and banged into it with a loud crash. The gate and bars jangled loudly from the impact. It did not seem to faze the gorilla. It held onto the bars of the gate and began shaking them forward and backwards, trying to get it open. Although it appeared to be fully functional, and a big animal anyway, the gorilla's arms were clearly more disproportionately larger than what one would find in nature. Cord and Alan quickly moved forward and began to regain their composure. Although it did not stop its show of rage immediately, the absence of an audience seemed to somewhat calm the gorilla down. They crept a little more cautiously down the hallway, trying to peek into the cells before they walked in front of them. As they approached another occupied cell, their hearts sank. Lying in the middle of the cell, with a grotesquely misshapen body, lied Joe the janitor. He was lying on his back, with his legs actually curled to one side, his lumpy feet almost touching the side. His arms were swollen and lumpy looking, as if he had knots under his skin. Although his head had some of the knots, his face was normal, except for the look of pain and sorrow. He let out another sorrowful moan. "Joe!" Cord exclaimed in a whisper. Cord placed his hands on the bars of the gate and began pulling. That familiar rush and euphoric feeling enveloped him, as his muscles bulged, overcoming him with a power that almost made him giddy. The bars he was holding bent slightly, and the gate gave a little. Through clenched teeth, Cord said "These cells were obviously designed to withstand strength applied from a performance-enhanced captive." Alan grabbed hold of the gate and pulled with Cord. The gate immediately pulled from the doorway with a clang, the pieces from the hinges and locking mechanism breaking and flying apart. "But not the strength of *two* captives." Alan said, slyly. Cord laid the gate to the side and walked into the cell with Alan behind him. "Joe, can you hear me?" Cord asked, as he knelt down beside him. Joe's eyes slowly opened. "Joe, listen - we're going to get you out of here." Cord said, as he motioned for Alan to go around and get Joe under his other arm. Alan walked around and knelt down and reached out. No sooner than they had laid their hands on him, he moaned in pain. "No! Don't move me!" Joe said frantically, with a hoarse voice. "I hurt somethin' awful. Any movin' makes it so bad I can't stand it. Besides, there ain't no fixn' what they've done to me." Joe said. It seemed to be all he could do, just to breathe and speak. "I'm glad you found the keycard I left you. Weren't long after that, that they took me and started doin' all kinds of experimentin' and injectin' me with all kinds of stuff. They *knew* I was talkin' to you." he said. His breathing seemed to be getting shallower. He winced and closed his eyes as he began speaking again. "You boys best be gettin' out of here 'fore they do the same to you." Joe said weakly. Cord and Alan could barely hear him. "Joe, when we get out, we'll send help, okay?" Cord said. Joe didn't answer. "Joe?" Cord said. Cord reached out, then hesitated, thinking about Joe's pain. He then cautiously placed his hand on Joe's misshapen shoulder and shook him gently. There was no response. Joe was gone. Alan and Cord sat there quietly for a moment and then rose to their feet. "This is even worse than we thought. We've got to get out of here." said Alan. As they walked out of the cell, they heard someone call their names in a loud whisper. "Alan? Cord? Over here!" A few more cells down the hallway, they found Mark Donovan. He was standing, holding on to the bars of the cell for support. His face was bruised, bloody and swollen. He was missing some of his front teeth. There was blood on his face and all over the front of his lab coat. "You were right! You were right about everything!" he said hoarsely. "Stand back." said Alan. Mark stumbled backwards, and placed his hands on his knees to support himself. Alan and Cord grabbed the gate and pulled it out of its frame. They went into the cell and each took one of Mark's arms to support him. They helped him out of the cell and into the hallway. They began stumbling up the hallway, back the way they had entered. "Listen . . ." Mark began, panting and breathing heavily. "They know you've got an extra keycard. They know you were in the medlab. They know *everything*." he said. Mark was doing his best to walk, but they were practically carrying him, with his feet stumbling and dragging the floor. Cord stopped and turned to face Mark. The effort of walking seemed to have Mark on the verge of passing out. "Mark?" Cord said. He lifted his head up, then dropped it back down, his chin bouncing against his chest. "Mark?" Cord said, louder this time, using his thumb and forefinger around Mark's chin to raise his head up. He did not speak, but his eyes were open. "Did you deliver the message I gave you?" His eyes closed slowly. Cord was getting ready to ask him again when he began speaking. "Yes. I found him and gave him the note that morning before I came back to the facility. Your friend said . . ." Mark's speech was slurred and his eyes closed once again. "Mark!" Cord said loudly. ". . . he said to tell you . . . that you could count on him . . . B F squared." said Mark. He started coughing and a string of bloody spit hung down from his mouth. The coughing actually seemed to revive him a bit. In spite of everything that they had been through and the grip of fear they were now in, Alan and Cord both grinned when they heard those words. "They came and got me that same morning when I got back to the facility. They almost beat me to death and told me that they knew I had been stealing some of the Stage I Enhancers. And they knew what you guys were up to." Mark finished, exhausted. "Who was it? Roberson?" Alan asked. "Yeah, and a couple of guys I've never seen around before." Mark said. They shuffled on up the hallway, staying as far away from the side that had the agitated gorilla as possible. "They know absolutely every move you make. I don't know why they haven't stopped you two, yet." said Mark, as they helped him through the doorway and back into the main hallway of Section 7. As they turned in the direction they had been initially traveling down the main hallway, they heard a voice. "Because I like to see my lab rats participating in practical real-world field exercises from time to time." There was no mistaking Roberson's voice. They saw a shot of sparks and heard a muffled *thump!* They felt Mark's body weight shift, and he sagged down toward the floor, falling forward. They held on to him, but quickly saw the large hole in the back of his head, revealing shattered gray matter, bone shards, and blood. Although the lights were low, they could see that Roberson was holding a smoking pistol with a silencer attachment on the end, still trained in their direction. He was actually grinning. He had 4 men with him who were fully suited up in assault gear. In unison, Alan and Cord each let go of Mark's arm and each hoisted up an empty animal cage and tossed them toward Roberson and his men. The hired guns stepped in front of Roberson to take the brunt of the impact, but they all still fell back like bowling pins. A couple of the men let out loud grunts. Cord and Alan heard Roberson scream *Take them alive!* They turned and began running down the hallway the way that they had come in. As they passed animal cages, they quickly used their hand and yanked them over, creating obstructions in the hallway that Roberson and his men would have to maneuver around in their pursuit. As they pulled down various cages, there were yelps and cries of startlement and fear from the animals that some of the cages contained. Alan could hear Cord say . . . *sorry, sorry, sorry* . . . each time he overturned a cage. Scared for his life, he still managed a smile and made a mental note to tell Cord about it later. *If we live.* He thought. As they reached the doorway, Cord had already taken the keycard out to beep the door. He waved it in front of the keypad, but nothing happened, save for a red light flashing and a negative-sounding buzzer. "He's already deactivated the keycard." Cord said in panic, looking at Alan. They looked back down the hallway. Roberson's men were shifting the cages Alan and Cord had dumped in their way as fast as they could. Fortunately, it was taking them longer to move them than the few seconds it took for Cord and Alan to knock them over. Alan quickly stepped up to the double doors and placed his hands flat against them, near the edges where they met. He grunted and pushed inward and outward, and the doors slowly slid out of the way. Cord ducked under Alan's arm, and then Alan hurriedly slipped in. The doors slid back together with a *smack!* They were back in the prep room for section 7. Not wasting any time, they sprinted over to the other double doors on the opposite side of the prep room, and together this time, they quickly forced the doors apart. As they slipped through the doors back into the medlab, the double-doors behind them beeped open, with Roberson and his men filing through into the prep room. With only seconds separating them and Roberson, Cord grabbed a fire extinguisher from the wall next to the double-doors. He held it around the neck with one hand and held it in the middle with the other and began banging the base of it against the keypad next to the doors. After his third contact with the keypad, it was smashed and gave off a satisfying shower of sparks and smoke. The double-doors slid open about two inches and stopped. They could hear Roberson screaming *Get it open! Get it open!* They began running haphazardly back through the maze of equipment and cubicles, pulling down some of the equipment as they went by. The equipment crashed down in sporadic piles, creating an obstacle course of expensive scientific equipment.

24

Wednesday, October 7th - 4:17 am

Jason peeped out the blinds and verified that both black sedans were still parked outside of the Carson's home. Faye and Robyn were sitting quietly on the couch. Little Cord and Hayley were both asleep on a blanket in the floor, in front of the TV. Jason thought that the air actually felt heavy to breathe. "Okay, get the kids ready. I think we need to roll." Jason said. They did as he asked. They all moved single file and hurried out to Jason's car. Robyn got in the back with Little Cord and Hayley, who Faye had in her car seat carrier. Faye got into the passenger seat. As the last door slammed shut, Jason already had the muscle car started and rolling back out of the driveway. Both black sedans' lights came on and they began pulling out, following the orange car.At first, Jason kept the car going the speed limit and obeying all traffic signs and lights. He was not going anywhere in particular at this time, because of the trailing sedans. Although they kept their distance back, they still kept pace with Jason and made no efforts to be secretive. He tried a few times to lose them from just maneuvering through a maze of roads in a couple of local housing developments. He sped up a little each time, but they matched his pace and did not lose him. He wasn't really trying all that hard at this point. He was just testing the waters.

Jason made his way to Interstate 85, and headed north, toward Charlotte. Although he had no doubt that he had the upper hand in the horsepower department with his souped-up muscle car, and traffic conditions were light this early in the morning, he really did not want to open it up to lose the sedans because of the unpredictability of the other vehicles on the road. He pushed past 100 mph in several places, but the sedans stayed right with him. He had the option of hitting the break-down lane to pass traffic, but at this point, felt it was an unnecessary risk with the families in the car. Both children were sleeping again, and the women were silent. He finally caught a little break as he approached one of the exits for Belmont, a little town between Gastonia and Charlotte. There were three lanes for northbound traffic. They were in the far left lane with the sedans behind them. The exit ramp was on the right. There was a clump of cars that occupied all three lanes. As they got close to the exit, Jason accelerated, jumped in front of the other cars in the other two neighboring lanes, and darted back across all the lanes, making the exit just in time. Only one sedan succeeded in following them. The other could not get over. "Ha! Ha! One down!" Jason exclaimed. They pulled up to the traffic light, which was red, at the end of the exit and stopped. The remaining sedan pulled up behind them. The passenger door opened, and a man in a suit, wearing dark sunglasses, jumped out and began running toward them. He was holding a gun in his hand. "Hold on!" Jason said. He pushed the gas pedal down to the floor and smoke boiled from the rear tires of the orange car. He shot through the red light, narrowly averting a crash with a pickup truck. The man ran back to the sedan, hopped in, and they began pursuing once again. Jason did not hold back anymore. He ran red lights, stop signs, and cut through parking lots. Although the big, heavy sedan could not stay right on his tail, he could not seem to get it out of his rear-view mirror. Both children were awake now. Hayley's eyes were wide with wonder at the motion of the car's acceleration and the swinging back and forth as it cornered. Robyn spoke to her soothingly and patted her little chest. Faye was unable to attend to her, as she was in the front seat, hanging on. Little Cord's eyes were also wide, as if he was deciding whether to cry or not. Jason saw his little head pop up in the rear-view mirror, as he sat up straight from having been asleep. "We gonna beat 'em in this race, ain't we boy?" Jason said, with his voice as level as possible. Little Cord looked around and saw how fast they were going. "Yeah, let's get 'em." he said. "Whee!" Robyn said as delightfully as she could as they cornered hard. Surprisingly, Hayley nor Little Cord, did not start to cry. He yanked the steering wheel and headed into the parking lot of a home improvement store. He was gradually gaining ground as he would weave in and out of rows of parked cars, until someone unexpectedly began backing up, right in front of him. He layed down on the horn, and the car pulled back forward into its space. The delay was enough for the sedan to get right back on his bumper. He floored the gas pedal once again and headed around to the rear of the store.

"This is unit two. The subjects are still all together in the vehicle from the unexpected guest. They are continually evading contact and are causing a commotion that will surely attract undesired attention. Unit one was cut off in the pursuit, but they have been notified of our position and they are en route. How do you wish to proceed?" said the passenger of the pursuing sedan into his hand-held radio. There was a pause of a few seconds before a voice crackled back over the radio. "Unit two, designated subjects are now considered designated targets. Unexpected Guest is to be considered a target as well." said the voice on the radio. "Roger." said the sedan passenger.

As Jason rounded the store, his heart sank. The loading dock area was a mess, and vehicles, including tractor trailers, were parked awkwardly. He drove right into an area with the loading dock on his left, and vehicles and pallets of lumber in front of him and to his right. There was absolutely no way through. The driver of the sedan, which was right on his tail, realized that Jason was trapped. He yanked his wheel to the left, and then backed up to block his retreat with the side of the car. Jason rolled halfway into the clearing and stopped. "Hold on!" Jason exclaimed. He threw the car in reverse and stomped the gas. 600+ raw horsepower shot the muscle car backwards and dead into the passenger side of the sedan. There was an explosive crash of metal to metal, crunching plastic, and shattering glass. All the occupants of the orange car bounced and jerked with the impact. Both children began crying loudly with fear. Robyn quickly began rubbing and talking soothingly to Hayley, as she hugged Little Cord with the other. Faye was clamoring to the backseat, between the two front seats. Robyn unfastened Hayley and passed her to Faye, and they each were speaking softly to their children, trying to calm them down. Jason quickly rolled down his window, pondering the next move. The driver of the sedan, looked over at his passenger. The airbags on that side of the car had deployed, but they evidently were not enough, as the sedan passenger was down for the count. The driver, who was only shaken up, and bruised from the airbag deployment got out of the car and pulled his silencer-equipped gun from the shoulder holster under his jacket. He walked over to the driver side of the orange car. "Game's over." he said loudly, as he began to raise the gun to point it at Jason. Jason moved faster. He quickly raised and fired several shots from his 25 caliber pistol through his open window. The man jerked from the impact of the shots and stumbled backwards, falling on the pavement. "And you lost!" Jason exclaimed.

The loud repercussion of the gunshot brought fresh cries of fear from the children. The women did their best to try and calm them down. Jason had to restart the muscle car, as it had shut off from the impact. It actually dragged the sedan with it for several feet, before it pulled away from the side-crumpled vehicle. From having pulled the sedan, it actually left enough room for them to get by. Jason thought better than to go to his own home, but headed somewhere that he thought would be a temporary safe haven – his parent's house. Since his parents were out of town, he would not be putting anyone else in danger.

25

Wednesday, October 7th - 5:03 am

Just as Alan and Cord approached the door on the opposite side of the medlab, the same one they had entered earlier to get in, it opened up. They both stopped running. At first, both men had relief sweep through them. Into the medlab stepped Doctor Strausburg. He made eye contact with them, and oddly, had no look of surprise, or even the slightest change of facial expression. They both prepared to start running through him, toward the door. But then, as if in slow motion, there were some large figures falling in line behind the doctor, and entering the medlab. Four unbelievably large men that would have made a Greek muscle god look like one of their little brothers. They immediately recognized House as one of the men. They were all about the same size. 6 feet tall and 300 + pounds. Completely ripped. Although House looked like a relatively normal, but large, Caucasian blonde-haired male, the other three men each had some odd attribute or a disproportion that seemed to detract from their humanity. The brown-haired goliath whose head was as big as a basketball, and he had a neck to match. The red-headed man's skin looked as if it was thick and calloused all over. The black giant had hands that seemed almost double their proportionate size for his body. Doctor Strausburg stepped aside, and the four monsters continued walking toward Cord and Alan. The men were staring in horror and fascination at the four approaching man-towers, before Alan finally grabbed Cord's arm and pulled him back down to Earth. "Let's go!" Alan yelled. They turned to run. They could not go back the way they came, due to their obstructive equipment trail leading back to Roberson and other men with guns. They headed North through the medlab, where Mark had led them before. They continued pulling equipment over until they realized they were wasting their time. The huge men were tossing the equipment aside more quickly and easily than they could drop it in front of them. They just kept running. It did seem, at least, that they could run faster than the behemoths.

They finally reached the door that Mark had taken them in the other night. It had the place to swipe the keycard and the numeric entry keypad. They both pulled, pushed, banged, and rammed the door with their shoulders. It would move under their efforts, but it would not give. They were both pushing against the door when there was a sudden booming crash as they both felt a wall of flesh smash against them. They found themselves lying on top of the door in the floor, inside of the area they had been trying to get in to. House had hit them like a freight train. He had flown over them with the impact. He stood up and began walking toward them. They could see the other three giants through the doorway, headed toward them.

Both of them were sore but they scrambled to their feet. They knew that impact would have probably killed someone who was not on the enhancer. House grabbed Alan's arm. "Don't let 'em pull you in close, Cord!" Alan yelled as House swung him around, crashing him into a cabinet on the wall. Cord backed away from the doorway as the other three giants filed in one at a time. They were not in any hurry. The black giant stepped up to Cord, who backed up to the wall. "Can't we just talk about this?" Cord asked feigning a smile. The man swung his oversized fist into Cord's stomach before he could even raise an arm defensively. Cord grunted loudly as his body was actually driven part-way into the wall behind him. The man grabbed one of Cord's arms and yanked him back out of the wall, and sent him stumbling around into the arms of the thick-necked giant. Cord forced his elbow back as hard as he could into the man's stomach. The man grunted with surprise and released him. Alan gained his feet and ran full steam into House. "Gohh." Exclaimed House as Alan hit him, knocking him to the floor. The red-headed man came up behind Alan and grabbed him in a bear hug. Alan twisted and turned furiously until he slipped out of the hold. Cord had turned to try and get to Alan when the thick-necked man grabbed him and actually lifted him into the air and threw him toward a desk and chair. Cord landed on the desk and bounced like a rag doll. *We're going to die here. They're just playing with us right now.* Cord thought, as he rose painfully from the desk.

He looked around. The four giants were just standing there, watching them, as if giving them a little breather before they began again. The room was full of settling dust from all of the destruction. Although both men knew they were being toyed with, none of the giants had any hint of a smile or any other facial expression for that matter. He looked over at Alan. He was bleeding from several cuts. Cord looked down at his own body and saw that he was bleeding as well. He again looked at Alan, who was looking back at him with a defeated look on his face. Cord wondered if he had that same look on his own face.

The giants remained motionless as the dust finished settling. Roberson walked into the room. They could see Doctor Strausburg with some of the other thugs that had been with Roberson just outside the doorway. "Well, just think, gentlemen . . . if you would've just gotten with the program, you two could have easily beaten all four of these guys. *And* the other four that came with me. No matter. We've still collected some valuable data from your use of the Stage I and II enhancers. So, even having to make you disappear and considering the damage done in the lab here, you two were not a total waste. We still got what we needed." said Roberson. "There's no way that we can just disappear without someone knowing and figuring this out." Cord said. "We've got families, friends, co-workers . . ." Alan said. Roberson interrupted. "We've been handling it just fine for quite a few years, now. We've become very adept at making people vanish. We've taken care of the disappearance of people far more noticeable than you two average schmucks. We do whatever it takes." he said smugly.

He paused and then continued. "Oh, and by the way, your families and your friend in the hotrod are all dead." He lied, with a big smile on his face. "You low-life . . ." Alan began yelling expletives as he lunged for Roberson. Cord leapt at the same time, with a loud roar of sorrow. All four giants moved swifter than one would think such large bodies could, and intercepted Cord and Alan before they reached Roberson. Standing side-by-side, their arms, legs, and fists were rapidly flying and landing blows on the four gargantuan human beings as both men fought with hot rage at what Roberson had said. Unfortunately, the goliaths, who were much bigger and stronger, quickly had them beat down to the hard floor. They continued pounding the two men, who were both on the floor in fetal positions. Cord and Alan could not deflect the onslaught of blows, so they tried their best to keep their faces and heads covered from the rain of them delivered by not only fists and feet, but also the chairs, file cabinets, a copy machine, and whatever else the behemoths found handy. They became entombed by a pile of equipment and furniture as the four large men continually slammed things upon them, as if making a cairn for the men's final resting place using office equipment instead of stones. Once they were covered, Roberson commanded the giants to stop.Three of the giants dispersed, but House appeared to be unhappy with having to cease the beating, and grabbed one of the tallest, heaviest cabinets in the room, picked it up and slammed it down on the top of the pile before he walked away. Roberson didn't seem to mind this delay of his command. He walked over to the badly beaten men and had to roll over a copy machine, which clunked to its side on the pile, and then pulled out a chair, which he tossed aside, to reveal both of their bloodied, bruised, and contorted faces. Anyone who had not been on enhancers would have surely already been dead from this severe of a beating. They appeared *to be* on the brink of death. "Oh, no, gentlemen. I'm not going to *kill* you . . . at least, not right now. We've got some other things from other divisions we can test on you two since you're no longer interested in participating in our performance enhancement study." He kicked Alan, simply because his leg was sticking out from under the pile, lying closest to where Roberson was standing. Alan screamed in pain, surprised by the force of the slim man's kick. Roberson chuckled and then turned and walked back toward where Doctor Strausburg was standing, just outside of the office. Alan and Cord could barely hear what Roberson was saying to Doctor Strausburg. "Alright, Doctor, get some propofol and dope those two up. Get someone to haul them back down to section 7, lock them up, and then start cleaning up all of this mess from here to there. I've still got to go deal with their families. I don't know how in the world four grown men with guns still haven't taken care of one man with two women and two children." he said. The statement struck terror in Cord and Alan's hearts, but also gave them a sense of relief and hope. Roberson left the medlab. Doctor Strausburg directed Roberson's four hired soldiers to begin cleaning up in the medlab first and to leave the two men in the room under their pile of rubble undisturbed. "If there is any equipment that has sustained damage, we will dispose of it. If it is obviously undamaged, please place it to the side." Doctor

Strausburg said in his thick accent. The soldiers shouldered their weapons, and began cleaning up in the medlab. Doctor Strausburg turned to House and said "You four wait here in the medlab. I will need your help in getting those two out of that pile of wreckage and down to section 7 after I have administered their propofol shots. Do not go back in there to remove *anything* until I have given them their shots and the propofol has taken effect. Do you understand?" asked Dr. Strausburg. House nodded. "I will be back shortly." he added and then walked away.

Although Cord and Alan had both been drifting in and out of consciousness, they kept hearing a voice trying to keep them awake. It was only a whisper, but it seemed out of place, considering their given circumstances. Cord forced one of his swollen eyes open. He blurrily saw a familiar face surrounded by long, curly, sandy-blonde hair peering at him through the hole in the wreckage pile where Roberson had pulled a chair out from in front of his face. Her eyes were wet with tears. He knew he had to be dreaming. "Alan, are you still conscious?" Cord asked weakly. "Yes." He heard Alan respond hoarsely. "So, I'm not dreaming?" Cord asked. "If you are, we're both having the same one." said Alan. "Listen closely, you two. There's not much time. I'm trapped in here, too. I can't get any word out for help. Roberson has changed the codes and has the whole place locked down where only he and Strausburg can get in and out through the secured doors using their keycards." said Andrea Lawson. "Andrea, what are *you* doing here?" Alan asked, looking at her through the hole left by the toppled copy machine. "I don't have time to explain. Just know that with our given circumstances, we've only got one chance to get out of this." she said, holding up the two syringes full of swirling, glowing liquid. "The nanobots?" Cord asked. "Yes. If Roberson or Strausburg get to me now, they'll do the same thing to me as they're planning to do to you two. Your bodies have been conditioned with the enhancers and are ready for the nanobots. It'll either work . . . or . . ." she trailed off. "Or It won't . . . but we might die some horrible death anyway." Cord finished her sentence. Andrea nodded. "Let's do it." Alan said.Andrea knelt down and maneuvered her shaking hand through the opening in the wreckage to Alan, while holding the syringe. She shoved the oversized needle into his neck, which was the only place she could reach, and emptied the contents of the syringe into his system. He winced and stifled a yell. She did the same to Cord. No sooner had she began pulling her hand back through the opening, she heard footsteps crunching over some scattered bits and pieces of broken glass behind her. She subtly left the syringes in the pile of debris and turned around, facing the sound of the footfalls. It was Doctor Strausburg, who now stood over the kneeling Andrea. "Ahh, Doctor Lawson. You are bright and early to work this morning, aren't you? The early morning hours seemed to have confused your sense of direction, no? The medlab is a long way from section 1, Doctor." he said with his thick accent. "I was just coming down to get some enhancer . . . what happened in here?" asked Andrea as she began to climb to her feet. Doctor Strausburg completely ignored her question. "Nonsense, Doctor. Everything that happens in this facility goes by my desk. There are no trials on schedule this week." he said. "I know . . . I was going to get some to keep in my office . . ." she began again. "Doctor, we both know that not only do you *not* give the injections yourself, but it is against policy to keep the enhancer outside of the medlab." said Doctor Strausburg. "I was getting it for Doctor Donovan." she said quickly. Doctor Strausburg stood silent for a moment and then smiled. "Do you not think we haven't known of Doctor Donovan's use of the enhancer since day 1? If he would have needed enhancer for a participant, you can bet he would have come down himself, so that he could put an extra one in his pocket. No matter . . . Doctor Donovan is no longer with us here in the program." Doctor Strausburg said. Andrea was getting ready to speak again when Doctor Strausburg held up his hand, as if to quiet an unruly child. "No, Doctor Lawson, I do not think I believe anything that comes out of that pretty little mouth of yours." said Doctor Strausburg. Andrea felt fear slowly seeping into her and spreading across her face. Strausburg smiled and backhanded her.

Alan felt like he was beginning to cook from the inside out. He broke into a severe sweat. Whereas his body had finally become numb from the beating he had received, it suddenly began to hurt everywhere again. Cord's reaction was the same. Although the pain seemed to climb toward the unbearable mark, it gradually took a nose dive and not only did it begin to subside, but he actually started to feel *good*. He could feel his swollen eyes going back down. He opened them back up, and his vision was clear. It seemed even better than before. Although both men could hear the conversation between Andrea and Doctor Strausburg, it was like they were in a daze. Their bodies were going through a metamorphosis, and although they were feeling better moment by moment, they could still barely move. Their minds were also hypnotized by an experience that they could never explain. Alan was able to bend his head down toward his shoulder, to look at the rip in his flesh he had sustained from being hit with the corner of some piece of equipment. The pain had been replaced by an intense itching. He saw the red irritation around the gash, fading. The wound itself began healing at an incredible rate, right before his eyes.

Andrea began backing away as Doctor Strausburg began walking slowly toward her. "House! Come here, please!" Doctor Strausburg shouted. The massive man walked into the room. "I believe we've got a third guest for section 7. Please get her and hold her, so that I can give her an injection as well." said Doctor Strausburg. Doctor Lawson had backed into a corner and had no-where to run. She tried to dart past the walking wall of flesh, but House easily grabbed the woman, and turned her around in his arms, where she was facing Doctor Strausburg. The doctor approached her as he pulled the syringe from the vial. He raised the syringe needle-side-up, thumped it a couple of times, and pushed the plunger just enough to get any air out of it, squirting a minuscule amount of the liquid out. "I'm just going to give you a little medicine to make you sleepy." he said in a patronizing tone, as if she was a child and he was her pediatrician - not a lunatic with a doctoral degree.

Roberson used the tag number from the orange muscle car provided by one of the men who had pursued it, to find out who the owner was and their current address. With his connections, he also pulled up current addresses for Jason's family and some of his other affiliations. He printed out the list and stuck it in his pocket. He made a secure phonecall from Doctor Strausburg's office in section 3 and a short time later, met a black sedan, much like the other vehicle that had pursued Jason and the two men's families. This time, Roberson was going along to make sure the job was done right. Roberson directed the men to Jason's current address, which was about twenty minutes from the facility. When they reached the address, there was no sign of the orange car anywhere in the vicinity. The two men, with Roberson behind, went to the front door of the town home. One of them inserted a device into the lock on the door and very quickly had the door open. They searched the home and found no one there. Once back in the car, Roberson directed the men to the next address on the list: Jason's parent's house. As if suddenly released from a distant, foggy grip, both men's heads cleared and their bodies' range of motion kicked in. With a newfound rush of adrenaline, backed up by years of research and development poured into those tiny marvels known as nanobots, their freshly repaired and rejuvenated bodies exploded out through the pile of debris that had been weighing them down. Pieces of equipment and furniture rained down throughout the room. Doctor Strausburg snapped around, facing the men, the unused syringe still in hand. Alan and Cord kicked wreckage from around their feet and legs, as they began to move forward toward Andrea and her two captives. House released her and she scrambled to get out of the way.

Doctor Strausburg turned toward her. "You gave them the nanobots!" he exclaimed. Before he could turn back around, Doctor Strausburg already felt himself lifted into the air. Alan tossed him onto the pile of wreckage that he and Cord had just escaped from as if he was rearranging a pillow on a couch. The doctor screamed as his body dropped facing-up, against the awkward, jagged edges of the pile of debris. The other three giants ran into the room with the four soldiers behind them. House lunged for Alan, who was closest to him. The other three giants propelled themselves toward both of the men. The four soldiers held back, but un-shouldered their weapons. As House connected with Alan, Alan grabbed onto him and swirled around, using his momentum to propel House into the nearest wall, head-first. His head actually sank into the wall, as Cord's body had earlier. "Ooomph!" House grunted with the impact. The black giant's huge hands quickly closed around Cord's arms, holding them to his sides, like a clumsy child grabbing a Teddy bear. The giant with the large head and neck veered off toward Alan, while the red-headed one, with the thick, calloused skin maneuvered toward Cord and the black giant that had grabbed him. Thick-skin held both of his hands together and raised his massive arms over his head, making to bring them down against Cord while the black giant held him. Just as his arms dropped, Cord bowed forward, pulling the black giant with him and causing the blow to strike the black giant instead of himself. The black giant stumbled to the side from the impact, releasing Cord from his grip. Cord moved forward toward the leathery-looking red-head and began jackhammering blows from his fists into the man's stomach and chest. The man was staggering backward as Cord pushed forward. Cord delivered an uppercut into the man's chin, which brought the giant down.

Basketball-head steamed forward and head-butted Alan, propelling them both into the wall behind Alan, where the impact left Alan's body print in the wall. Alan quickly recovered from the jolt and drove his elbows into the back of the giant, who was still pushing against him, as if trying to drive him through the wall. The giant yelped in pain as his upper torso dropped from the blow. Alan then brought one knee up into the front of the man's head so hard, it flipped the giant back onto the floor, crashing into the debris. House had finally pulled his head from the wall and staggered to his feet. The huge-headed giant pulled himself up from the floor. His face was covered with the blood that was still pouring from his nose. He wiped his face with his arm and looked down at his own blood as if it was the first time he had ever seen it. He looked back at Alan and let out a howl of rage as he began to lurch forward. House leaped toward Alan at the same time.

As the leather-skinned giant fell, Cord suddenly felt himself falling too. The large hands of the black giant had grabbed around both of his ankles and yanked his feet out from under him. Since the giant had his legs from behind, he fell forward and was afforded the luxury of at least buffering his impact with his forearms. Once down, the giant began dragging Cord back toward him. He shook his legs and kicked his feet, but could not get loose from the awkward grip of those massive, strong hands. As Cord, who was face-down on the floor, began to try and turn over, he suddenly felt both of his wrists become enclosed, just as his ankles were. Leather-skin, who was bleeding from the mouth, had already begun recovering from his fall and had come to assist Big Hands. The black giant stood up while still holding around Cord's ankles. They had Cord held up in the air between them, as he squirmed around, pulling and shaking, trying to wrench himself free.

House and Big Head reached Alan at the same time. In the split second he had to react, Alan could see no clear solution. If he concentrated on any one of the two giants that had rushed him, it would leave the other one free. If he tried to get both of them at the same time, it would divide the power he could put into the assault. He swung both arms outward in an arc and managed to contact both giants in their stomachs. Although he had good, solid, satisfying contacts and was rewarded with grunts from both of them, they both, however, were also able to grab the arm that had hit them. He had known this scenario was possible, but this was all he had at the moment. He struggled to shake loose, but they held on tightly. He began to use his powerful legs to push forward in an attempt to pull away, but the giants began pulling his arms behind his back awkwardly. This caused intense pain which made Alan stop struggling for the moment.

The four soldiers had been watching the fighting, as if they were at a friend's house, watching a TV match. They had been grunting, laughing, joking, and pointing the whole time. They had made no move to interfere as long as the situation seemed to be under control. The commander of the four had checked Doctor Strausburg when the fighting had temporarily moved away from the debris pile. He pulled the unconscious doctor into the medlab and then used his radio to call Roberson. He also told Roberson about the presence of Doctor Lawson. "I am dealing with another situation right now. Get all three of them to level 7, each in his own cell. Check Strausburg's pockets, he should have the keycard you need. Once you get those three detained, please began getting that place cleaned up. This whole mess has costed us considerable time and money. We've got to get back on schedule." Roberson said. Jason parked his car behind his parents' home and ushered everyone in the back door as quickly as possible. The kids had long since calmed down and were back to their normal, cheerful selves as if they had not even been in a high-speed car chase and a shootout. Jason led them to the safest room in the house. "Okay, y'all stay put in here and don't come out. I know it's hard not calling the police on this, but we don't know who we can trust right now and who might be listening on the phone. I don't think it would have mattered if we would have tried going to a public place. They still would have come at us. At least here, I got access to my Daddy's guns." said Jason. The girls shook their heads and sat down, each pulling their kid onto their lap. "I'll be right back." Jason added and walked from the room. He came back holding two guns, a pistol and a 410 shotgun. He placed the pistol on the table near where they were sitting. "I think we're gonna be fine here, but these are the last resort." he said, as he propped the shotgun next to the table.

One of the soldiers began walking across the room to get Andrea. He walked near where the two giants held Cord up in the air, by his hands and feet. Cord exerted all of his strength and pulled his feet in, bending his knees toward his chest. He also pulled his upper torso forward, as if he was doing a crunch in mid-air. The two huge men held tightly to him, but both of them stumbled closer to each other from Cord's pulling. Suddenly, Cord kicked his feet out and arched his torso back. It was like the release of energy from a huge, coiled spring. The back of Cord's head contacted with Leather Skin's face with a loud crack. At the same time, his feet exploded into Big Hands' chest. Leather Skin fell backwards, covering his face as he howled in pain. Big Hands was also propelled backwards from the impact of Cord's feet against his chest, where he collided with the soldier who had been walking by. Big Hands landed on top of the solider, who grunted as the heavy giant landed on him, forcing the air from his lungs. Cord fell toward the floor, but twisted in mid-air, and much like a cat, landed on his hands and feet. In the few seconds of commotion, Alan felt the grips that both giants had around his arms relax ever-so-slightly as they watched their comrades get pelted by Cord. That slight reduction of the clamping pressure and a little drop of their focus was all Alan needed. He tensed his arms and twisted in place with a sudden burst of power, pulling his arms free from Big Head and House. While facing Big Head, he quickly delivered a forceful uppercut to the huge-headed man's chin. He heard teeth break and crackle as Big Head yelled a twisted cry through his disfigured jaw and mouth. In the same moment of the punch to Big Head, Alan employed a little of the martial arts he had actually learned from Ken Harrison, the skinny red-headed man who had taught he and Cord some of the techniques. He spun around and pulled his leg inward, cocking it as he did so. As his target came into range, he fired his leg out, contacting his foot into House's mid-section. House was propelled backward as if he had been hit with a wrecking ball. He screamed and had his hands on his crotch before he even hit the floor. Alan thought it was ironic that this giant had been brought in initially to help them learn the art that he had just used against him.

The black sedan pulled slowly down Jason's parents' driveway and stopped within 100 feet of the house. The two hired guns got out of the front of the vehicle and Roberson got out of the back. The three of them walked down the remainder of the driveway to the house. Roberson and one of the men stopped, while the other man continued to walk, heading to the rear of the house, with a pistol drawn. A moment later, the man with Roberson placed his hand up to his earpiece and then turned to Roberson and said "The car is here." Roberson's eyes narrowed as he smiled.

The three soldiers that were still standing, had quickly pulled their weapons from their backs during the brawl between the two men and the giants. They had their weapons trained on the two men, alternating back and forth between them. Cord quickly snatched up a small table from the wreckage and strategically hurled it toward them. The table smacked into two of the soldiers, flinging them backward onto the floor. The remaining soldier fired a burst from his weapon, which propelled Cord backward, crashing back into the debris pile. "No!" Alan yelled. "Nobody move!" the soldier shouted. Ignoring him, Alan ran over to where Cord had fallen and knelt down beside him. There were three bullet holes across his chest and he wasn't moving. Andrea came from where she had crouched during the commotion and knelt down as well. She felt the side of Cord's neck. "I can't feel a pulse." she said. She began clearing a spot next to him, to prepare to begin CPR. "You do the compressions, I'll do the breaths." she said. The soldier had walked up to where they were kneeling beside Cord. "You two, get up and let's get going." he said, motioning toward the door with the automatic rifle. Alan quickly grabbed the rifle and yanked it from the soldier's hands. The soldier lurched forward with the rifle from the pull of the shoulder strap, until the strap broke. Before the man could pull back, Alan swung the rifle against his head like a baseball bat. There was a sickening *whack* and the soldier simply fell over without even an utter. Alan tossed the rifle aside.

"Ohhhh . . . " Cord said, grunting, as he sat up. He pulled his shirt up and looked down at his chest. The bullet holes were already looking like freshly healed wounds. All three of them had eyes wide with wonder. "Amazing." Andrea said. There was one deformed bullet lying in his lap, which Cord picked up and held where Alan and Andrea could see. He looked around and could not find any evidence of the other two slugs. "Where are the other bullets?" Alan asked. "I don't know. I guess they're inside of me. How did this one get outside of me, though?" Cord asked. "My guess is that the bullet that you're holding in your hand was close enough to the surface of your skin that the nanobots were able to direct it and push it back out of you. The other two may be 'cordoned off' by some nanobots and antibodies. They may actually be dealing with getting rid of them as we speak. They might very well end up in your waste or something. I don't know the extent of their capabilities and programming." said Andrea. "You mean I might end up crapping the bullets out?" Cord asked, grinning. Andrea nodded. "There's a good joke there, somewhere." Alan said. He extended his hand and pulled Cord to his feet. "So, we're like invincible?" Alan asked. "Oh, no. I know this is truly fantastic, but there is only so much the nanobots could possibly keep up with. They can obviously rebuild damaged tissue, but they will have limitations on how much they can repair and how fast at one time. And the complexity of the tissue they repair, such as brain tissue. Don't let your guard down." Andrea said. She walked over to the motionless body of Doctor Strausburg and retrieved the vials of propofol and the hypodermic syringes. Cord found the soldier who had taken Strausburg's keycard and removed it from his pocket. Not entirely sure of every downed man and giant's vital signs, Andrea injected all 9 of them, doing her best to guess at dosages. The three of them then proceeded to the entrance of the facility. They went to Andrea's SUV in the parking lot. As soon as they cleared the gate, Cord used Andrea's cell phone and called Jason.

"Hello?" Jason answered. "Jason, are you and our families safe?" Cord asked. "They are for now." he said. "Thank God." Cord said, giving the thumbs up to Alan. "But, look . . . they found me. Some of those goons just pulled down the driveway." Jason said. "Where are you?" Cord asked. "I'm at my Dad and Mom's place." Jason said and gave Cord the address. Cord repeated the address to Andrea who punched it into her GPS. "We're on our way." Cord said. "I don't know what kind of junk y'all have got stirred up, but these scumbags have done tried to kill us one time today." Jason said. "Jason, thank you for taking care of our families." Cord said. "Oh, you know it, partner. I'll do whatever I can. Hey, I got to go. One of 'em just walked around back. He's carrying a gun." said Jason. The connection went silent. "Jason?" Cord said. Alan was looking at Cord with growing fear in his eyes. "They're safe for the moment, but some men just got to his parents' house and they've got guns. We've got to hurry." Cord said. Andrea was already driving as fast as the car would go. She retrieved the cell phone back from Cord and called someone and gave them the address. "Who did *you* call?" Alan asked Andrea. "I *am really* a scientist, but I actually work for the FBI. They recruited me and trained me just for this assignment. They have been on to Roberson for several years. They created a fictitious dossier and history on me that was a perfect match for one of the many skilled professionals Roberson needed to work on the program. This is the closest we've ever gotten to him." she said. "I thought the government already had their hands in this project?" Cord asked. "Oh, they do. There *are* crooked people in the government, too, you know." Andrea said sarcastically. "So you've actually been working on this illegal program as an undercover agent?" Alan asked. "Yes, I guess you could say that. The part of the project I have been working on for the past several years is perfectly legitimate. I've had to be careful in my snooping, because Roberson only had his most trusted personnel working on the other parts of the project." she said. "And what about Mark Donovan? You know he's dead, right?" Cord asked. "Yeah," She began with a sigh. "I really liked Mark. He checked out clean. As far as the FBI knows, he was just a doctor hired to work on the project, and had no knowledge of the corruption and plans for the use of the illegal research and illegal parts of the study. Of course, he knew of the other research, but I'm sure he had no idea that it was illegal. I assume that he just figured it was the advanced levels of the program. Of course, he had to keep the research information confidential, anyway. In many ways, Mark was actually more resourceful than I was. I knew he was juicing . . . you know, using the enhancer. Somehow, he had been able to get access to some areas that I still had not been able to get to. I tried to warn him away from messing around without giving away any information that could blow my cover." She finished.

Jason hurried from the front of the house to the back, carrying a 12-gauge pump shotgun, pumping the slide, loading a shell into the chamber, as he went. He peered out the blinds on the back door, and saw the man looking at his car. The man was only standing about 20 feet from the back door, next to the car. He had his hand on the side of his head and his mouth was moving, as if he was talking. Jason assumed that he was communicating the fact that he had a visual on his orange car. Already knowing what these men were capable of, Jason wasted no time. He raised the shotgun and leveled it, pointed it at the man, and aimed through the window of the door. He squeezed the trigger, immediately pumping the slide and firing again, following the fall of the man with the aim of his gun. The window of the back door exploded outward.

Although this man was wearing a bullet-proof vest, apparent from the fact that there was no visible trauma to his chest, it did nothing to protect his neck and head, where the majority of the pellets from the buckshot were directed. There was a spray of red all over the man's upper body as his neck, face, and head was tattered from the pellets. Jason chambered another shell as he backed away from the door and retreated back into deeper cover inside of the house.

Roberson and the remaining hired gun were startled by the blast from the shotgun. The hired killer put his hand up to his head and spoke. He waited a moment and then spoke again. He looked at Roberson and shook his head. They both quickly took cover from being out in the open. No sooner had they began to move, there was some shotgun blasts from one of the windows on the house, narrowly missing the men. "Go get him!" Roberson exclaimed. The other hired thug quickly made his way to the back of the house, leaving Roberson in the safe cover of a group of trees.

The henchman only had to slightly shove the back door to get it to open, as it was in a sad state due to the blast of the shotgun Jason had fired through it. He carefully crept into the house, being careful not to present himself as a target. Jason had not seen the man leave the cover of the trees, but he heard the scraping of the broken back door opening. He cautiously headed back in that direction. As he approached a hallway, he paused. Before he stepped out, he extended the barrel of the shotgun out into the hallway. There was an immediate response of plaster chips flying from the corner as bullets pelted it. He pulled the gun back and stepped back. Knowing his parents' house well, he knew where the best vantage point was for seeing down this section of hallway. As soon as the shots ceased, Jason quickly and quietly dropped down onto the floor and swung around the corner from floor-level and fired, more from instinct than from visual reference. Just as he had known, the man had been trying to use the bookcase at the other end of the hallway for partial cover. The blast of pellets hit home. The man howled in pain as he tumbled backward onto the floor. Jason jumped up and rushed to where the man had fallen. Jason looked down at the man who could not hold his gun, because his hands and forearms were ripped up by the buckshot. The man was frantically trying to help one arm with the other one and vice-versa, without any luck. He looked up at Jason, with a pleading look on his face. "This just ain't your day." Jason said, as he shook his head and fired another blast from the shotgun.

Jason quickly retreated back the way he had come, toward the front of the house. As he turned the corner of the next hallway, his heart sank. The front door was standing wide open, with the doorknob, deadbolt, and striker plates lying in the floor. Someone smashed right through it. He turned in just enough time to see the man with the raised gun. He barely had enough time to leap to the side, tuck and roll. He could hear the *Thump! Thump!* of bullets being fired at him from the silencer-equipped gun the man was carrying. He even heard the *Thwack! a*s the bullets popped through wall and floor behind him. He felt a searing- hot pain in his right arm and immediately knew one of the bullets had hit its target. He could not hold onto the shotgun as he came out of his roll, but he had quickly scrambled to his feet, and darted back down the hallway with jerky, zig-zagging movements, so as to better his chances of not being shot again. Thankfully the man pursued, as it brought him away from the room where the families were hiding.

The large SUV was sliding to a stop in the driveway as Andrea applied the brakes. Alan and Cord had already had the doors open and were getting out of the vehicle before it had completely stopped. Cord remembered what Jason had said about someone going around to the back of the house, so he headed that way. Alan saw that the front door was smashed and standing open, so he headed to it. Andrea put the car in park and then retrieved a handgun from her glove box. She jumped out and followed Alan into the house.

Cord rounded the side of the house just in time to see Jason sprint through the back door into the backyard. He was holding his upper arm with his left hand. He barely had time to dash around to the other side of his car and stoop down when Roberson came running out the same door. He came to a stop and looked around slowly. His attention focused on Jason's car. He knew it was as far as Jason could possibly have gotten in the short span of seconds from coming out of the back door. Roberson began walking slowly toward the car, cautiously stepping over the man Jason had gunned down next to it.

Alan and Andrea went in different directions inside of the house. Alan went forward, and Andrea veered off to the left. Alan began to hear voices coming from the rear of the house. He headed in that direction. Andrea slowly and cautiously opened doors that she came to and looked in. As she opened the furthest door at the end of the hallway and peered in, she found the two families crouched together, both women holding the guns Jason had left, nervously pointing them at Andrea. Andrea slowly raised both of her hands. "I'm here with Cord and Alan. They've come to get you." she said. Their faces were washed with relief, but neither woman faltered or lowered the weapon they were holding. From elsewhere in the house, Alan heard Andrea exclaim "Alan, I found your families! They're safe!" When Faye heard Alan's response "Thank God! I'm looking for Cord and Jason." She lowered her weapon and nodded to Robyn that it was okay to also do so.

Roberson was about to step around to the rear of the car where Jason had crouched down. "Roberson!" Cord shouted. Roberson stopped dead in his tracks, and turned to face Cord. He had a smug, irritated look on his face. "You're done." Cord said. Roberson raised the gun and pointed it at Cord. "I don't think so." he said. "Look, the FBI has been on to you for a long time. Why not stop now, instead of getting any deeper? It's over." Cord said. "It's never over, as long as there are people willing to pay for the technology that I've refined. And believe me, they are willing to pay. The potential for power and control is too tempting. You have no idea who all the players in this game are. Our own government is one of them." said Roberson.

Alan followed the sound of the voices as they got louder and louder as he approached. He saw the smashed back door and heard the voices coming through. He recognized the voices as Cord and Roberson. He quickly and quietly stepped through the back door. As he walked outside, he was only fifteen feet behind Roberson. Cord saw Alan come out, but did not acknowledge him for fear of giving away his position. Alan saw that Roberson had his gun trained on Cord while they were talking. Alan quickly looked around and saw the only thing available to possibly help him was a barbecue grill. He snatched the grill up and propelled it with all of his strength toward Roberson. Although Roberson caught sight of the flying grill in his peripheral vision, he was not fast enough to move out of the way. The grill hit Roberson hard and smashed him against the orange sports car. The impact was enough to actually propel him *inside* of the car through the window. "What's the matter, Alan, you didn't like the burgers?" Cord asked. "The burgers were just fine, I really just didn't like the dinner guest." he replied. "You're just a regular chef on steroids, aren't you?" Cord added. They both chuckled. They walked around the car to where Jason was crouched down. He was applying pressure to his wound, but his sleeve was covered in blood. "Andrea is with our families Cord, and they're fine." said Alan. "Thank God." Cord said. "What you boys done got into now? I know . . . *somehow* . . . this has something to do with Cord saving a nickel on protein or some other bull." Jason said, shaking his head. The three of them laughed as they helped Jason to his feet. "It's a long story." Alan said. "How's that arm?" Cord asked. "It hurts like crazy." Jason said. "But I don't think the bullet hit the bone. I got the bleeding to stop." He added. They walked into the house through the tattered back door.

Jason led Alan and Cord to the room that he had left their families in. "It's us. Everything's fine." Jason shouted through the door. Andrea opened it and the three men entered. The two men rushed to their families and embraced them. After everyone had settled down, Alan introduced Andrea to Jason. They all then headed outside. Andrea led them to her large SUV, and assisted Jason into the passenger seat, and then seated herself in the driver's seat. The large SUV had three-row seating. Cord and his family got into the back. Alan and his family got into the middle section. Andrea started the SUV and began to back up. "I guess the first thing we need to do is get you to the nearest hospital." Andrea said to Jason, smiling. "Yeah, that'd be good." Jason replied, matter-of-factly. They could hear the sound of sirens approaching from the distance. "Well, Andrea, here comes the back-up you called." Cord said. "Better late than never." Alan said. Without warning, there was a loud crash into the side of the SUV, into the driver's side, lifting it up and then dropping it back down with a bounce.

The impact startled everyone, and the children began to cry. There was another impact, this time the vehicle was raised completely up and clunked down onto the passenger side. "Maybe that back-up ain't too late." Jason said. Although no one was hurt, everyone in their prospective seats were piled on top of each other from the vehicle being on its' side, as no one had yet fastened their seat belts. They clambered around to upright themselves as the families tried to calm their children. Before anyone could begin to make an ascent toward the upper side of the vehicle, Andrea exclaimed "Oh, No!."

Through the spider-webbed cracked windshield, she could see Roberson standing in front of the overturned SUV. She could see the twisted look of rage on his face. His suit was tattered and bloody. Through his torn habiliments, she could see his large, sculpted muscles, no longer disguised by his expensive suit. She could see the heavy rise and fall of his chest from his breathing. It was him that had overturned the SUV. "It's Roberson! He must be on enhancers!" Andrea exclaimed.

"Seeing as how I'm the administrator of a multi-million dollar research program, it would only make sense that I would reap the benefits of some of our more successful endeavors, wouldn't it?" Roberson exclaimed rhetorically, as he rammed his fist into the hood of the SUV, causing it to spin on its side. Little Cord and Hayley, who had still not stopped crying from Roberson's initial impact on the vehicle, burst into fresh tears and wails of fear. "That does it." Alan said.

The passenger door on the topside of the SUV burst open and flew through the air from being ripped from its hinges as Alan shot through the opening like a bullet. He landed on his feet next to the vehicle. A moment later, Cord had moved from the back of the SUV to the middle and launched himself through the same doorway, dropping to the ground, next to Alan. The two men approached Roberson slowly and cautiously. Other than a narrowing of his eyes, the only other movement from Roberson was the rise and fall of his chest from his breathing. As they were almost within arm's reach of Roberson, he suddenly lurched forward and grabbed Cord's arm and jerked him down onto the ground. Dragging him on the ground, he yanked Cord past himself, then swung him upward, in a circular motion, and brought him back around from behind his back, slamming him back into the ground again. Cord cried out in pain. Roberson then did a spin-kick, directing his foot into Alan's stomach. Alan grunted loudly as he was propelled backwards in an upward arch. The path of the arch ended in an impact against a tree. Alan then fell over, with a grunt, as he had almost lost consciousness. Roberson looked around and scanned the immediate area, as if searching for something. He then walked over toward the SUV.

"Is everyone okay?" Andrea asked. The children were still crying, but their mothers had checked them out. "We're fine, just shook up and scared." Faye said. "Same here." Robyn said. "My arm still hurts from you sittin' on it." Jason said, sarcastically. Andrea shifted her weight and looked at Jason and rolled her eyes. "What can we do?" Robyn asked. The sirens were growing louder. "Help will be here soon. I think it's safest to just sit tight for now." Andrea said, but she had her pistol drawn and ready. The SUV moved slightly and there was a loud popping and clanking sound from the bottom of the vehicle. Roberson had ripped the drive shaft off. Gun in hand, Andrea began climbing up the front seat to the driver's door window. She pressed the auto window down button, and the window slid into the door. She then pulled herself up and out through the window. Jason tried to follow, but his arm had begun bleeding again and it was extremely painful to move it. He just could not climb with his wounded arm.

Roberson walked over to Cord, shaft in hand, and stood over him, looking down at him. "I see you boys have managed to get your nanobot upgrades after all. That's just fine. It might just take me a little longer to kill you two." he said as he kicked Cord in the side so hard that he half- tumbled, half-slid across the ground, over next to where Alan lay. Cord heard a sickening cracking sound come from within himself. The pain his body was feeling at the moment was excruciating. Roberson then walked over to where the two men lay. He lined the end of the shaft up with Alan's head, and brought it up as if he was getting ready to swing a golf club. "Fore!" he yelled.

"Drop it, Roberson!" Andrea yelled. Still holding the shaft in the air, Roberson turned his head back, toward Andrea. "I mean it!" she shouted. He lowered the shaft, but did not drop it. "Oh, no . . . a gun. Somebody help." he said without feeling, placing the back of his free hand up against his forehead, feigning fright. He began walking toward Andrea. "I *will* shoot you. Stop and drop the shaft." she said. He did not stop, nor did he drop the shaft. Andrea had leveled the gun, pointing it directly at his chest. As Roberson came into almost arms-reach of her, she fired a single shot. The bullet hit home, and there was an immediate stain of blood on the front of his shirt. He had a look of terror in his eyes, and he dropped to his knees, letting the shaft fall and roll aside. Andrea cautiously walked forward. Roberson's eyes rolled back and he fell face-forward and lay still. Andrea approached him and knelt down, still holding the gun, keeping it pointed at him. Her hand was shaking as she reached toward his neck to feel his pulse. "Boo!" Roberson said softly as he reared back up on his knees. She open-fired and kept pulling the trigger even after the gun was empty. All of the shots went into

Roberson. He had a sinister grin on his face. She began scrambling back to her feet as he popped up onto his. "You can't kill me, you naïve girl!" Roberson yelled. Andrea turned to run. Before Roberson could make a move to pursue, he found his legs taken out from under him. The shaft had smashed into Roberson's legs with a sickening smack. Without even a single cry of pain, Roberson rolled around on the ground and turned himself around. He saw Alan holding the shaft, as Cord was getting to his feet, right behind him. Roberson, although bloody in various places on his body, hopped right up from the ground as if the impact of the shaft on his legs had been nothing more than a scratch. "I see you two have got a little fight left in you." he said with an arrogant smile. Roberson turned to see three vehicles coming down the driveway. "Looks like I'm going to have *a lot* of work to do and messes to clean up." He added, his smile never faltering.

The back-up had finally arrived. A black SUV and two large, black sedans quickly pulled down the driveway and then off of it, into the yard, parking side-by-side. Andrea rushed to the passenger side of the SUV, where a tall, lanky man, wearing a black suit got out of it. She immediately began explaining the situation to the man, as he nodded in confirmation. Other FBI agents exited their vehicles. Barry Masters, the supervisor, immediately dispatched two of the men to assist getting the families and Jason out of Andrea's overturned SUV. "Barry, I emptied my gun into Roberson. Unlike when Cord was shot, it didn't even faze him. I believe we've missed something along the way. We're dealing with more than just the performance enhancements and nanobots here." she said to her supervisor.

The two agents escorted Jason and the two men's families to one of the sedans. The car started, and it began pulling away. Cord walked up beside Alan. Their eyes were filled with relief as they watched the sedan carry their families and their friend away. As they were watching the sedan, Roberson rushed at them. Alan swung the shaft, but Roberson intercepted it with his left hand and yanked it from Alan. The sudden movement sent the shaft spinning away. He followed through with his forward momentum and clothes-lined both men. As the fighting amongst the three men began to wind back up, the agents drew their guns and trained them in the direction of the ruckus. Barry directed his attention to his men and raised one hand. "Men, it seems that our handguns will be ineffective against our target, Daniel Roberson, the man in the tattered suit. The other two men are friendlies that *can* be harmed by firearms. Do not use your guns and stand-down unless I instruct you to do so, *or* you are directly defending your own life. We're going to have to think of another way to take down our target." he said.

Cord and Alan pulled themselves up off the ground. "He's just messing around with us right now, Cord. He's friggin' fearless." Alan said. "How can one man be so much stronger than the two of *us*? He's got to have more than just the enhancers and nanobots at work, here." Cord said. Alan nodded. "You can't kill everyone, Roberson!" Alan shouted. "Yeah, it looks like I'll just have to settle for killing you two for now. Then, I'll take my leave and go around tying up loose ends at my leisure." Roberson said, smiling. This time, the two men rushed at Roberson. Cord was in the lead. Unexpectedly, right before they got to their target, Cord made a dive and hit Roberson's legs, grabbing onto them. As Roberson and Cord grappled, Alan grabbed one of Roberson's ankles and one of his wrists and snatched him from the ground. He began quickly spinning around in a circle using centrifugal force to keep himself from Roberson's grasp. Around and around Alan went, faster and faster, until he finally released Roberson. Roberson flew through the air, over the house, hitting the chimney and breaking right through it. Bricks exploded and sprayed out toward the back of the house. There was a loud crash from the impact of Roberson's landing. Cord jumped up from the ground and he and Alan rushed around the house, with Barry, Andrea, and the rest of the FBI team trailing behind them.

Cord was the first to arrive behind the house and see the gaping hole in the side of the utility building, where Roberson had smashed through it on his descent. He rushed right into the building through the ragged opening. Alan was only seconds behind him. As Alan entered through the opening, he saw that Roberson, who was sitting in a pile of wreckage, already had Cord down and in a head-lock and was choking him. Alan glanced around and spotted a shovel, which he grabbed. He swung the shovel as hard as he could against Roberson's head. There was a loud and forceful *Thwang!* as the shovel contacted Roberson's head. The handle of the shovel broke and splintered. Cord and Roberson tumbled over. Roberson released his grip on Cord. Both men scrambled to their feet. Cord was infuriated, massaging his neck and coughing. He looked around quickly and spotted a surveyor's bush-axe, with a long, sharp banana-blade. He snatched the axe up and rushed at Roberson, who had his back to the wall. "Let's see those nanobots repair this!" Cord yelled as he brought the axe down toward Roberson's head. Roberson had time to bring both of his arms up in a defensive posture to protect his head. The axe sank into Roberson's arms with a sickening *Thunk!* There was a slight spray of blood, but the axe did not go through his arms. Cord quickly pulled the axe back, revealing dents along the blade where it had contacted Roberson's bones. With a look of astonishment on his face, he swung the axe forcefully down once again. The axe again, stopped at the bone, but this time a piece of flesh about four inches long popped off of one of Roberson's arms from next to where the first cut had been made. The missing flesh revealed bone which was of a shiny, silver nature. As Alan and Cord stared in horror and awe, they could see the real-time action of his flesh regenerating over the shiny bone. Just as their bodies were now equipped, there was literally a swarm of thousands and thousands of tiny nanobots crawling around, busily rebuilding and reconstructing the missing and damaged flesh at a remarkable rate. Roberson slowly lowered his arms from the defensive position and shifted his gaze back and forth between the two dumbfounded men. A smile spread across Roberson's face as he delighted in the amazement and fear that he was sure the two men were feeling with their new-found knowledge: Roberson was virtually indestructible.

"Oh, you're absolutely right, Cord. I do have nanobots, just like you two. Along with a titanium-alloy endoskeleton, and a few other improvements from some of the many other projects we are working on. This amazing technology could have been given to you two as well, in time. If only you had not worried about trivial things and focused on a greater vision." Roberson said. He snatched the axe by the blade from Cord's numb hands. He swung the axe toward Cord's neck. "Cord!" yelled Alan. Alan had already snapped out of his daze, and grabbed the back of Cord's shirt and yanked him out of his paralysis and back from certain decapitation. Roberson began an assault with the axe, swinging it quickly in long arcs, left and right, toward the two men. The men were stepping back quickly, barely avoiding the slicing blade. As they began to approach the opposite wall of the utility shed, Alan shifted his path so as to pull away from Cord and create two targets for Roberson. As Cord was closest to the wall, Roberson pushed forward, concentrating only on him. Alan began scanning the area for another weapon. It seemed that there would be nothing that could be useful against Roberson. To make matters worse, Alan watched helplessly as Cord tripped over some junk lying on the floor.

Cord fell backward, landing on the pile of junk he had tripped over. Roberson raised the axe above his head and actually leaped forward as he began bringing it down, so as to put all of his body weight and energy into the swing. Cord frantically felt around on the floor for something to try and deflect the blow. He knew his own bones were not made of metal. There would be no regeneration of a severed body part. As Roberson and the blade began coming down, Cord barely caught the blur of Alan rushing in behind him. Alan jumped up in the air and literally looked like he was getting ready to slam-dunk a basketball. There was a blur of a red arc coming down from Alan's hands toward Roberson's head. Cord's hand found something and closed his fingers around the cold, smooth object and quickly brought it between himself, and Roberson with the falling axe. It was a large wrench, and Cord grabbed the other end with his other hand. The red, plastic gas can burst open as Alan drove it down on Roberson's head. Gas spewed, gushed and sprayed everywhere, but mostly soaking Roberson, the target. Alan kicked off of Roberson's back and pushed himself back from the spray. As the axe-blade contacted the wrench, there was a loud clank of metal-to-metal, and a spray of sparks. The sparks ignited the gas vapors and Roberson burst into flames with a loud *whoomp!* Cord kicked up into Roberson's torso and the flaming man crashed into and was propelled through the utility shed wall behind him.

The group of FBI agents moved as one, began backing up, as the flaming Roberson burst through the wall of the utility shed. Alan and Cord came sprinting out of the shed prepared to continue their fight, only to find Roberson standing in the yard, furiously, but uselessly, slapping at the flames that covered his head and most of his torso. Oddly, he made no cries of pain, but he could be heard cursing at the flames. They saw the appearance of nanobots surfacing, then they would burn and drop away as if clumps of melting plastic. His movements became slower, and the slapping of the flames became pitiful attempts at patting them out. His flesh had grown dark and was peeling away in places. The nanobots were not able to keep up with the speed at which his flesh was being burned away, and they themselves would burn when they appeared. The flames began burning brighter, and with more intensity as the fire began to spread down his legs. He turned around in a circle as if searching for something, and then began trudging slowly toward Jason's parents' house. His footsteps seemed to get heavier as he walked. He then stopped and slowly dropped to his knees about ten feet short of where there was a garden hose coiled up and connected to a spigot on the brickwork of the house. There was a sickening and crackling sound as he slowly turned his head and looked directly at Cord and Alan. His entire body had been completely engulfed, but now the flames were subsiding. He was completely black and charred. Although his eyes could not be clearly seen, both men could feel the cold, hateful stare that came from that hot smoldering face. After a moment, his head loosely, wobbled around back in place as he fell forward, his body slumping to the ground. It twitched for a few moments, and then the smoking corpse remained motionless. Alan and Cord cautiously approached the body. Cord nudged the charred remains with his foot, half-expecting the man to get back up again. "Stop, drop, and roll, dummy." Alan said. Cord looked over at Alan, who had a dead-serious look on his face. Alan redirected his gaze to Cord. The two men looked each other over. Their clothes were dirty, tattered, and raggedy. Their faces and every part of their bodies that were exposed through their torn clothing were either dirty or had streaks of someone's dried blood on their skin. As serious as the situation had been, both of them began laughing hysterically and couldn't seem to stop.

26

Monday, November 2nd -
9:00 am

ONE MONTH LATER
FBI BUILDING - WASHINGTON, DC
DEBRIEFING

"Okay, it's great to see you gentlemen again. This time with no crazy, power-hungry lunatic trying to kill you." said Barry Masters, as he walked into the conference room and closed the door behind him. He shook hands with Alan and Cord. "You guys have done a great service for your country, and I believe you deserve to know whatever we can tell you about what you were involved with. Of course, you are under an order of secrecy, and certain pieces of information are classified and cannot be discussed." He added. Both men nodded in agreement. "Andrea, can you get us all up to speed?" Barry asked. "Well, as you know, the facility on South Boulevard has burned to the ground. Our Hazmat Team is going through everything and salvaging whatever can be saved. There was a lot of valuable research that may not be recoverable." she said. Barry nodded and said "You do know that the government was involved in this research, but there are always a few rogue employees who want to try and take ownership of the work and sell years of this research to the highest bidder, with no consideration for what it may be used for. By no means did your government support anything beyond the stage I enhancers you were initially given. The unauthorized implantation and human testing of the batteries was just the beginning of the illegal research that we were trying to uncover. Speaking of which, Andrea, have you made arrangements to take care of having these men's implants and nanobots removed and get them a complete physical examination to determine their health and any adverse effects of the enhancers and so forth?" Barry asked. Andrea nodded. "Yes, their pre-evaluation shows that they are both in perfect health. I've got the paperwork orders for the battery implantation and nanobot removals right here." she said, holding up an official document. "Very good. As far as we know, all of the people involved with Project Nemesis have been apprehended . . . including the ones in our own government. We have gone to great lengths to track down as many missing persons and their families that were involved with the project as possible, to bring them some closure. We have also back-tracked as far as we could to erase as much public knowledge as possible of this *clinical study* business that Roberson had, trying to recruit guinea pigs. I think, for the most part, we've got the situation contained and out of the press and public eye." said Barry.

"All of Daniel Roberson's holdings were seized . . . well,

all that he didn't have in Swiss accounts or off the radar. The families of all the missing persons have been compensated. It's little consolation compared to the loss of a loved one, but we're fighting evil every day." Andrea said with a sigh. "What happened to the people at the facility?" Alan asked. "The legitimate employees that were not involved with the illegal activities have been reassigned. Everyone that was there when we left that day perished in the fire." she said. "That's ironic, Roberson dying from fire, also." Alan said. They all nodded. "What was the deal with Roberson's abilities, anyway?" Cord asked. Andrea looked at Barry questioningly, who nodded back to her. "Roberson had his hands in many different baskets. He took advantage of anything that would make him more powerful . . . that is, physically, and financially. Once technologies were proven safe and with minimal risk, he would be quick to use them on himself. He didn't want to be one of the guinea pigs to be studied, poked, prodded, and tested. That's where the people like you guys came in. From our studies of Roberson's body, he had many enhancements incorporated into it. Performance enhancers, nanobots, and a titanium alloy endoskeleton, just to name a few. He had also found a way to re-route some of his nervous center functions. That's why he seemed impervious to pain. Although you guys had a much higher pain threshold than before, due to the in-troduction of the enhancers and the rapid rebuilding of your neural pathways by the nanobots, his body was registering the sensations, but sending them as informative signals, rather than excruciating pain responses. This technology could be very useful in many different applications. Unfortunately, we could not extrapolate enough data from his ruined body to quite understand how it worked, and no data has yet been found at the South Boulevard facility or any of his other known places of operation." Andrea said. She paused and then added "You know, he just may have killed us all that day if he would have had the foresight to wear a flame-retardant suit - or had come up with a way to make his body fireproof." She finished. "I'm sure that was probably in his plans, somewhere." Cord said.

It was a beautiful, sunny day in Washington DC. The three friends walked down the concrete steps that led down from the FBI building to the street. There was a limousine waiting to take Alan and Cord to their hotel, where their families were waiting on them in the nicest suites available. There was a shiny, orange, 1991, fully restored, 600 plus horsepower muscle car sitting behind the limo. Jason was leaning up against it with his legs crossed. Andrea walked up to him and put her arms around him. "How's that arm?" she asked. "Doin' just fine, thanks to you, honey." he said in his loud, redneck drawl. Alan and Cord walked up to where the couple was embracing. "Good grief, enough of the PDA. Do that in private." Cord said, half-jokingly. Jason and Andrea released each other. "Oh, I've got the best room money can buy . . . thanks to you two clowns." Jason said. The four of them started laughing. "You never thought one of your classic money-saving schemes would end up working out like this, did you?" Alan asked. Cord opened his mouth to reply when they all heard a terrifying scream. They glanced over at the intersection closest to where they were parked. A mother, pushing a stroller, had just began pushing it up the handi-capped ramp at the curb when her toddler broke away from her and was running back into the intersection to retrieve a dropped baby doll. Alan and Cord leaped over the limo and were in the intersection in a flash. There was a blare of horns, the screech of brakes, a loud thump of impact, followed by another frightened scream.

Jason and Andrea watched a car slowly slide to a stop right next to the limousine. Alan had the little girl held to his chest with one arm, with the other extended out onto the front of the car, his hand on the bumper. Cord had both of his arms extended, one hand on the hood, the other on the bumper. As the car came to a stop, Cord and Alan stood up. There were dents in the car where the men's hands had been placed. The men had been sliding backward to slow the car down, and the friction of their feet caused smoke to come from their shoes. The mother came running up, carrying her infant in one arm, tears pouring down her face. Alan gently passed the crying little girl over to her mother. The mother kept saying *thank you* to the two men over and over as she covered her crying little girl's face and head with kisses. She then hugged her two children tightly and began rocking them soothingly. Cord and Alan began walking back to where Jason and Andrea waited. Andrea had spoken to the driver of the car and given him her number to have the car's dents repaired. "We'd better get out of here. I'll straighten out the paperwork for this incident later. It's awesome to be able to help people, but you two are going to have to try to figure out how to keep a lower profile for now." Andrea said. Cord halted, as he remembered something. He turned around and walked back over to the mother, who was still crying and gently rocking her children. He placed a hand on the little girl's shoulder and she lifted her face from her mother's neck. He pulled the baby doll from his back pocket and held it in front of her tear-streaked face. She immediately stopped crying and reached for the doll. The mother stopped crying, and even the little girl's baby brother settled down. The little girl rubbed her eyes and then smiled at Cord. He smiled back. He then turned and walked back to where his three friends were waiting on him. They were all wearing smiles. Jason got in the driver's side of his orange muscle car. Andrea walked over to the passenger door and opened it. As she was standing next to the open door, she looked down at the piece of paper she had carried out of the FBI building and stared at it for a moment. She then ripped it in half, crumpled it up into a ball, and tossed it into the backseat of the car. "I'll burn that later." she said. She looked back at the two men, smiled, pursed her fingers to her lips, said *Shhhhh.* and then gave them a quick wink as she entered Jason's car.

Withhold not good from them to whom it is due, when it is in the power of thine hand to do it. – Proverbs 3:27

It was in 2009 that my co-worker and totally awesome friend, as you will know him by the name of *Alan Carson* in this book, noticed me huffing and puffing while I had bent over to tie my shoelace. I was 195 pounds, and not in a good way. He said something along the lines of *Man, why don't you come with me and try out my gym one day? You can be my guest.* So I did. That part of the story is true. *Alan* is the inspiration for this novel. In three short months, with his help, advice, guidance, and push, as far as diet, exercise, and supplements go, I managed to drop 45 pounds! I felt better than I ever had in my life, including when I was a younger man. Although he joked about me being a big cry baby, he was surprisingly patient, and he didn't just teach me the routines, he taught me a lifestyle. I kept it up for almost ten years, and then had some ups and downs with plateaus, depression, and now most lately covid-depression. I found out just how real depression is. I used to think that allergies were a joke, until I started all the sneezing, having watery eyes, and plain misery as I got older. As I gained more muscle mass during the "good" years, I did some research and found that the average male in my current age group could bench-press 3 reps of 80% of their body weight. Because I had been pushing myself so hard, I ended up needing dual inguinal hernia surgeries, and once I had to go to the emergency room because something had *popped* in my head during some of my heavy bench pressing. I had to be more careful. But, I did manage to bench press 2 reps of 300 pounds. I only weighed 150 pounds. According to my math, that was 150% stronger than the average male for my age and weight at that time for bench pressing! I knew there were much stronger people out there than me, but I was very proud of my accomplishment. It was very hard work and required a lot of discipline for me to achieve this performance. I was thinking *There has to be another, easier way to do this.* As I researched additional supplements and ways to continue my success, I dug deeper into the science, and being who I am, I daydreamed of the mixture of science and science fiction. I hope you enjoyed Mark Donovan's explanation of how the body works because most of it is real science. I would also be remiss if I didn't mention my other co-worker and my BFF, as we fondly call each other. You will have known him as *Jason Kaiser* in the book. He is also a bodybuilder. He was also instrumental in supporting and encouraging me, not only in the sport of body-building but in a lot of life's problems as well. I must also thank my entire family for bearing with me during this time. I was a completely different person when I had transformed into the healthy, shapely man that I had been. Instead of just being prideful, I was cocky and a little arrogant. No one has to worry about that now, however. I'm still around 160 pounds, but now I have just an ordinary dad bod.

www.ingramcontent.com/pod-product-compliance
Lightning Source LLC
Chambersburg PA
CBHW061303210726
48293CB00003B/1097